I0541186

Hephaestus

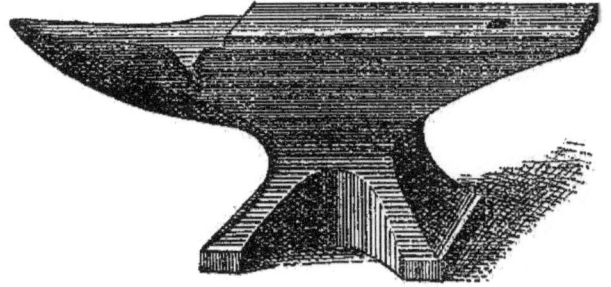

Hephaestus
a novel
thomas
tull

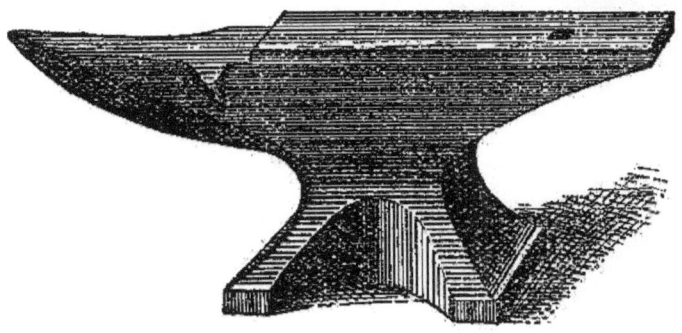

The Artless Dodges Press /
www.TheArtlessDodgesPress.com /
Cleveland, Ohio

The following is a work of fiction. Characters, names, situations, events, and locations described in this novel are purely the invention of the author's mind, or are used fictitiously. Any resemblance to persons living or dead is purely coincidental.

All Rights Reserved. Printed in the United States of America. No part of this book may be used or reproduced in any manner whatsoever without written permission of the publisher.

Hephaestus
a novel by Thomas Tull
ISBN 0981993958
EAN-13 9780981993959
copyright © 2010 Artless Dodges, Inc.
Published by The Artless Dodges Press
Cleveland, Ohio
www.TheArtlessDodgesPress.com

Cover design by T. Maven
www.TrashMaven.WordPress.com

"Qualis artifex pereo!"
("What an artist I die as!")

- Nero, Emperor of Rome (54 to 68 AD), before committing suicide with the aid of
his secretary.

Katherine

The first time I saw Katherine she seemed to embody everything I had ever hoped to find in another person, and I suddenly and irrationally had the sense that if I could just be with her then I would be happy in ways that nothing else could come close to. It was whatever you call love at first sight when you don't believe in love at first sight. I was twenty-one, and still finishing school. I'd already written the novel that I thought was going to make me famous. Katherine was eighteen but seemed much older than all the other girls in her class. Her family had money, and she'd gone to better school than the other girls and had spent more time at better parties with better people. I was working for one of the English professors, helping the freshmen with their composi- tions. I liked the job quite a lot. It was nineteen fifty-nine, and everyone was trying to write like Jack Kerouac. I was writing like Kerouac, too, although I told myself that it was only because that was the way fiction was supposed to be written. I wrote

like that, I told myself, because I agreed
with the ideology of his aesthetic. In real-
ity I was writing bad imitations like everyone else, but admitting that meant admitting
that the novel I'd written was just a bad
imitation, too. Katherine came to me with a
story she'd written about a girl who kills
herself by driving her father's car off a
bridge. It was a really terrible story, and
she said as much. I lied and told her that it
just needed some work, that it could be
really something if she just made a few re-
visions. That didn't interest her at all, so I
asked her instead where she'd gotten the
idea for the story. I told her that if I understood how she was thinking about the material then I could be more helpful. She
didn't know, though. She said that she was
just trying to write something dramatic. I
explained that death itself wasn't dramatic,
that drama happened in the story leading up
to the event. I asked her if she'd read a
bunch of books that she hadn't read. Then I
asked her if she wanted to go to a party I
knew about that weekend. She couldn't though,
because her parents were coming down and
she was going to spend the weekend with
them in the city. She told me that I shouldn't
worry about the story, that it was a waste of
my time to try to make it better, that as long
as she passed the class she'd be happy. She'd
only made the appointment with me because
the professor had told her that she should. I
said I was glad that she had. We were meeting

in the professor's office, and even though I wasn't supposed to I took one of the books I had mentioned off the professor's shelf and told her she should read it if she got bored while she was with her parents. She asked me wouldn't I get in trouble if the professor found out his book was missing? I told her that it was fine, that the professor let me borrow his books all the time, that I would just tell him that I had it. After she left I figured that with the way things went I would probably never talk to her alone like that again, that the book was gone, and that I would catch hell whenever the professor found out. But on Monday afternoon she brought the book back. She'd liked it, she said, but she wasn't sure that she understood all of it. She asked me if I could explain it to her. I told her that I could.

Two

At that time I was seeing a girl named Karen. Karen had graduated the year before, but had stayed around because she got a job working for a company nearby. It wasn't a very interesting job, and she didn't like it very much. Whenever we went out she spent the first hour complaining about the job and the place she worked. Then she would ask about all of her favorite professors and students I knew who were my age and younger who she'd known while she was there. I had been seeing her for a while and probably would have broken it off except that Karen had her own place. It wasn't a very nice place, but it not being very nice meant that nobody paid any attention to her and nobody cared what she did. There were a lot of artists and writers living in the building, and they were up all the time. There was always a record player or a radio on, or you could always hear someone talking through the walls no matter what hour you came and no matter how late you left. It was a real Kerouac kind of place and I think that's why I

liked it and I think now that that's probably a lot of the reason that I liked Karen.
Aside from the place where she lived and
what we could do there we didn't have too
much going on. We'd had a class together, and
one day we'd run into each other at a deli
across the street from the campus. I was
really jazzed about the class, and so I
started talking to her about what the professor had been talking about. It was a class
on eastern religions. I saw her there the
next day, too. We started having lunch together. Then one day she said she'd made
lunch for us, but that she'd left it back in
her room so she didn't have to carry it
around. She snuck me into her dorm and there
wasn't any lunch. Afterwards she said she
thought she had some crackers somewhere if I
was really hungry. Then it just never ended.
We'd go out to dinner or go see a movie and
fool around in the car. Then she graduated
and got her own place, and we just went
there. We didn't even go out anymore. We just
hung around with the people on her hall. I
wrote a lot of short stories and let everyone
on her hall read them, and everyone told me
the stories were really good. Everyone was
older than me, and they'd all read more books
than I had, and knew more about art, and so
when they said my stories were good I believed them. I thought that probably they
would think my novel was good, too, although
I didn't let anyone read that. I believed that

they would think it was good, and that was good enough for me then.

Katherine was seeing someone, too. I found out pretty quick. One of my friends saw us talking and told me to watch myself because she was seeing some older guy. My friend had seen them together when the guy came down to get her the weekend before, the weekend she'd told me she was in the city with her parents. I said that maybe it was her brother or somebody like that, and anyway that it didn't have anything to do with me because I wasn't interested. My friend said the guy sure wasn't her brother and that if I wasn't interested then it didn't matter.

Three

I was interested, of course, but I felt ridiculous about it. I didn't know her at all,
and so of course I wasn't going to admit that
I thought she could make me happy in ways
that nothing else ever could. For as much as
I pretended to be, I really wasn't all that
cynical about love. All my cynicism was borrowed from authors I'd read, and most of the
time I was able to convince myself that I
really felt that way. I think being with
Karen helped, because I could feel like what
we had was sordid and depressing and doomed,
even though the truth was I didn't care
about Karen and losing her wouldn't matter
to me very much. When we did break up I
found that I was sorrier to have lost all of
the people on her floor, sorrier that the
party was still going on without me, than I
was to lose her.

The breakup didn't happen until later,
though. While I was talking to Katherine I
was still seeing Karen. Katherine started
coming to see me when I was supposed to be
helping students with their compositions.

She'd sign up for a time slot and then stay for an extra hour, while one of the other students waited in the hall. She never had anything written, either. After the story about the girl driving her father's car off a bridge I don't think she ever wrote anything else. For a while I gave her books off the professor's shelf, and when we met again we would talk about them. Then she stopped reading them, but she kept coming to see me. We'd talk about whatever was going on. We talked about her family and I told her about mine. She told me about her boyfriend and I told her about Karen. I asked her if she loved her boyfriend and she said that she did and she asked me if I loved Karen and I said that I didn't, that Karen and I had no delusions about our relationship, and that anyway I didn't believe in love. She said that it was sad that I felt that way, and I told her that life was sad, and that believing in things like love was just a way to pretend that it wasn't. Love was a nice thing to believe in, I said, like heaven and God, but at the end of the day they were all just ways of coping with life's depressing finality. She asked me if that meant that I didn't believe in God either, and I told her that we needed God to exist far too much for Him to actually exist. At that time it was a bit of a shocking thing to say, and it really upset her. She said that if I didn't believe in anything nice, that if all I ever thought about life was that it was going to end, then

I should just kill myself because I wasn't really living anyway. I didn't have an answer to that, so I started talking about how not believing in God or thinking that life was meaningless was not the same thing as not wanting to live. I didn't really know what I was trying to say, and she didn't want to hear any of it anyway. She left and I sat there wondering why I had said everything I'd said. I imagined her going back to her room and calling her boyfriend, and him telling her what an idiot I was for thinking all of the things I'd told her I thought, and that of course love was real, and that of course he really loved her. The thought of it, of her telling him all the things I'd said, drove me absolutely crazy.

Four

Then my mom got sick, and I had to go home for a while. I talked to Karen on the phone a couple of times, but after two or three conversations we didn't have anything else to say to each other. I didn't know what was going on with any of the people back at school that she wanted to know about, and I didn't care about her job. I kept hoping to hear from Katherine, but then I talked to my friend, the one who'd told me that Katherine was seeing an older guy, and he told me she'd gotten engaged. She'd come into class showing everyone the ring. But about a week after that I got a letter from Katherine saying that she was sorry she'd gotten so upset with me, that she really missed talking to me, and that she really hoped my mother was feeling better. It was just a short letter, but all the same it was really nice to hear from her. I wrote back and told her how things were with me, and congratulated her on her engagement. What she wrote back really surprised me. Her next letter was all in response to my saying that I didn't believe in

love. She said that she could understand
what I had said about love being a reaction
to our awareness of our own mortality. She
admitted that, in all honesty, she wasn't sure
that she believed in God herself, and that
the idea of a heaven where people stood
around in white robes with everyone they'd
ever known had always struck her as
slightly absurd. She could understand, she
said, the problems that this presented, because without heaven then what did love
come to? If love wasn't forever then it wasn't
love in the way that she'd been raised to
think of love. The idea of soul mates, of being wed forever in the eyes of God, of love
being a union of eternal spirits, all went
right out the window. But this part of love,
this part that dealt with eternity, was only
part of love anyway, and if I wanted to dismiss this part then she was perfectly willing to dismiss it with me, and call it something not worth believing in. But, she wrote,
there was an awful lot to love that she
wasn't ready to dismiss, like wanting someone
else to be happy, like caring so much about
someone else that you stop caring about
yourself. She said that love was just a name
for the inspiration to be the best version of
ourselves that we could be, because we
wanted to deserve the life that was being
devoted to our own.

Reading her letter I was embarrassed because I'd never felt any of those things toward any of the girls I'd ever been with, and

it occurred to me that when I had talked to her about love I had been talking about something I didn't knew anything about. Katherine knew a lot more about it and understood it a lot better than I did. What I'd felt toward other girls was something else entirely. What I'd felt for Karen was certainly something else, although I'd entertained the illusion that it was love and was somehow tragic and beautiful and entirely befitting an artist like myself. It wasn't love I'd felt, just pathos, and all of a sudden I envied Katherine for what she felt and I envied the guy she was with because she felt it for him, and I felt certain that I had been right all along: that being with Katherine would bring me a happiness that nothing else could ever come close to. And, because I was home and there was nobody I had to be cynical and jaded for, I starting thinking about what a lucky son-of-a-bitch her fiance was, and how much happier I would be if I was him.

Five

I guess I was wrong about how happy he was, though, because in her next letter she told me that I was right, that love was just a fantasy, and that her fiance had called off the engagement. I'd spent so much time imagining what it would be like to be him that I had to read the letter over again to make sure I was understanding it right. It didn't make any sense. He'd been sent to California for work and when he came back he told her that he'd met someone else, someone who had opened his eyes to all that was possible between two people. He felt terrible about it, because he never wanted to hurt Katherine, but he knew that if he went through with the wedding he would be keeping both of them from the lives they could be living. He had to hurt her now and save her from the life they were moving into. She'd asked him why they couldn't have all that was possible between two people, and he'd told her that she was far too wrapped up in her father's world, which was the old world, to ever be able to see beyond it. He

didn't even sound like himself, she said. He'd
told her that she could keep the ring, that
he'd bought it for her, but she'd insisted on
giving it back, which seemed to hurt him and
which, she said, she was glad about.

   She'd been changed by the experience, she
said. She could see now that the love she'd
imagined was free from all illusions had
just been a subtler set of illusions and
dreams she hadn't realized were dreams until
they disappeared. I wrote back and told her
how sorry I was, and what a fool her former
fiance was, and how sad it made me to think
that she would give up on love because of
him, because I'd come to realize that she'd
been right all along. Then I told her about
Karen and about how we were through and
had never really been anything anyway, and
how I felt next to nothing about losing her
because I'd never really felt anything for
her in the first place. Karen and I didn't
have anything like what she and I had, I
wrote, and it was only finding someone like
her that made me realize it. Then I said that
if she was going to be home over the summer
that if she wanted I would take the train
down some weekend and take her out. I
thought about it for a long time before I
wrote it and then I decided what the hell
and wrote it and sealed the envelope before
I could change my mind. I figured I could
still always pretend that I had meant it in
a friendly way, all of the things about
never having had with someone what I had

with her, and taking her out, and that way
she wouldn't think I was trying to make a
move on her. But then she didn't write back,
and I figured that she thought I was trying
to make a move, and so I wrote another letter
explaining that I had only meant it in a
friendly way. After that I got a letter from
her saying that she was sorry I hadn't heard
from her for so long, that over the break
she'd been away with the parents on the
coast for two weeks and hadn't received any
mail, and that of course she would love it if
I came down to see her. After that I wanted
like nothing else for it to be summer so that
I could see her. Every time I got a new letter
I had to make myself read it because I was
sure that in it she would tell me how she
was seeing somebody new, and how great it
was, and how she believed in love again, but
with somebody else.

Six

She never wrote about anybody new,
though, and when summer finally came I took
the train down and we went out to dinner
and a movie. That was the first time I met
her parents, too. Her father made a big show
of shaking my hand, a big show of treating
me like his equal in a completely condescending way. Right from the word go I didn't
like him. Her mother was very proper and
very pretty for a woman her age. It was easy
to tell that she looked the way Katherine
would look when she was that old. They both
came to the front door to meet me and they
both sat down in the living room with me
while I waited for Katherine to finish getting ready. Katherine's father asked me what
year I was in school and I explained that I
was a senior or had been a senior and was
trying to finish the rest of my courses by
mail. He asked me what was keeping me from
my studies and I explained that my mother
was having some health problems. He asked me
what sort and I said they'd found a lump in
her breast, hoping that if I was blunt they

might have the decency to feel embarrassed about asking. They didn't, though. Katherine's mother shook her head and said how awful it was. She went into a long story about a woman she knew who'd had the same thing, and was now doing very well. Katherine's father watched Katherine's mother with a put-on air of interest, and I disliked him even more for it and for starting her on the subject.

Finally Katherine came downstairs. I don't know what it was about her, but every time I saw her I felt like she was the only thing that mattered. Right away she put on her coat, like she couldn't wait to get out the door. Her parents hadn't even stood up from the couch. They seemed surprised that she didn't want to come in and join the conversation, and I was secretly happy to see them caught off-guard and unsure what to do or say next. Then her father stood and shook my hand again, and told me to be back by eleven at the absolute latest, and I wondered why he'd bothered to treat me like an equal, even for pretend, when things were going to go right back to the way they really were between us.

I didn't wonder or feel annoyed about it for too long, though, because once we were outside and walking I didn't care. Katherine started talking about all of the things that had happened at school since I'd been gone, and I walked along listening and feeling happy and thinking about how happy I felt and trying to remember everything as it happened so that I could revisit it later.

After that I went down to see her almost every weekend. My mom was getting better, and all of my professors had written back saying that if I would just take the last test or write the last paper they'd give me a grade for the course and I wouldn't have to take it next year. I had already been working under the assumption that they would let me finish that way, and had a lot of the work done. When I was finished and the last paper had been sent my parents took me out to dinner, and Katherine came down for it, too. She hadn't met my parent, yet, and I was nervous and embarrassed by them and I kept telling them what to say and what not to say while we were waiting for her to arrive. My parents were nothing like Katherine's parents, and I was worried that when she saw that she would think of me differently. It had to do with class, but it was something else, too. My father had always been aloof, and I'd always secretly been proud of him for it. I loved the way that he didn't put on fatherly airs the way that other kids' fathers put on fatherly airs. When I met other kids' fathers I always felt like they were puffing out their chests or standing on their toes. My father didn't even seem to notice when I had someone over to the house. Also, he was always a little bit messy in some way. Either his shirt would be untucked or the buttons would be done up wrong, or

his hair would be all in a jumble. After the
depression it was like he decided that there
was nothing you could do if everything
could just fall apart like that, and so he'd
stopped trying. He'd managed to keep working
through those years, but that had somehow
made it worse. Going in day after day expecting to be fired, waiting for it to happen, had
totally burned him out. My mother was always
following him around, reminding him of
whatever was going on. When they first found
out that she was sick he broke down and
cried, right there in the doctor's office. My
mother ended up having to comfort him. It
was pretty funny, in a way.

I'd written a story about them over the
summer. It wasn't about them exactly, but it
was about people a lot like them. This couple
had a son, too, but he wasn't in the story
very much. In the story the couple finds out
that the man has prostate cancer. That's the
first thing that happens. The rest of the
story is the couple going home and going
through their routine. It's told from both of
their perspectives, and neither one of them
thinks about what the doctor said. The woman
thinks about how much there is to do around
the house, and about how helpless the man
would be without her. The man thinks about
the weather and what's going to happen the
next day. At the end of the story the son
calls to ask how they are, and they tell him
that everything is fine. I wanted to give the
story to Katherine. I thought that I had

really captured something about my parents. I wanted to be able to present them to her, because I was worried about how they would look if they only presented themselves.

Seven

But it was obvious right away that I didn't need to present them in any way, because my parents clearly adored her and she adored them. I gave her the story anyway, for her to read on the train. A few days later I got a letter from her saying that it was her favorite story and the best story she'd ever read. We went to the shore the next weekend and sat on the sand and she told me that when she was a child she'd been afraid of everything, and was always hiding in her closet or behind her mother whenever they went out. They'd come to the shore for a week one year, and she'd made believe that there was a house somewhere under the sea where she could go and hide from everything that scared her. For some reason that seemed like the final word. When I got home I asked my father for a loan so that I could go buy a ring. My mother wouldn't hear of it, though, because she had her mother's ring that she'd always hoped I'd give to the girl I wanted to marry. It was like something out of a movie. I took the train up that afternoon and sur-

prised her at work. She was working at her
father's company, answering the phones. When
I asked her she started to cry and stopped
answering the phone, and the phone kept
ringing. Finally someone came out to see why
she wasn't answering the phone and made a
big scene when they found out what had happened. Someone went to tell Katherine's father and he came out of his office, looking
self-conscious and a little annoyed. He saw
the crowd that was forming as more people
came out to see and so he shook my hand and
hugged his daughter. He sent someone out for
champagne and we had a party in one of the
meeting rooms. Katherine was crying and
showing everyone the ring, and people were
shaking my hand and telling me how they'd
worked at the company for so many years, and
how they'd known Katherine since she was a
little girl, and how lucky I was, and how I'd
better take good care of her, or there'd be
hell to pay from her old man. Then Katherine's father said that he would call his wife
and have her meet us, and that we should all
go out to dinner to celebrate.

Over dinner Katherine's father grilled me
about how I was going to provide for Katherine, and what I planned to do to support a
family. Katherine's mother looked apologeti-
cally at Katherine and then stared at her
food. Katherine told her father that I'd written a book that she was certain was terrific
because I was a terrific writer, and it was
going to sell a million copies. She didn't

know why her father couldn't just be happy
for her, she said. She left the table and went
to the bathroom and her mother went after
her without saying anything to either of us.
When they were gone Katherine's father
apologized and said that I had to understand, Katherine was his only daughter and
his little girl, and we had known each other
for so little time. I said that of course I
understood. He said he would just feel more
comfortable with the situation if we'd been
going together for a while, if we were really
sure that we would get along so well, and if
he knew that I had some sure form of income.
He asked if I had sent the manuscript out to
publishers and I told him no, that I was
still working to get it exactly as I wanted
it, and that I had been busy over the summer
finishing my coursework. He congratulated
me, then, for having completed my degree, and
asked if I had considered going back to
school to pursue a higher degree and go into
teaching, as he understood many writers did.
I told him that I hadn't thought of it, and
that anyway my financial situation was
strained enough by the cost of my under-
graduate studies. It pained me to admit it,
after he had made such a point of telling me
I couldn't afford to marry his daughter. But
instead of saying anything about it, he said
that if I was willing to postpone the wedding until I finished a secondary degree
then he would be willing to help me with the
cost. It could be a lot of money, he said. And

if afterwards we still wanted to get married, then we could do so with his blessing.

It wasn't what I was **expecting** to hear. Katherine and her mother were coming back across the room and so he said that I should think about it and talk to Katherine and then give him my decision. Then Katherine and her mother were back and we didn't talk anymore about it. Katherine looked like she had been crying and her mother, bolstered I guess by her desire to defend her daughter, told Katherine's father that the dinner celebrating the engagement was not the place for such conversations, and that she didn't want to hear another word out of him unless it was kind and supportive. Katherine's father said that of course she was right, with the same false air of equality he'd had shaking my hand the first time we met, and congratulated us both and told the waiter to bring champagne.

Eight

After that everyone seemed to have a pleasant enough time, but all I could think about was what her father had offered me. It was an awful lot of money, and I liked him even less for offering it. I'd felt all along that teaching was a failure in itself. Teaching was what you did if you weren't a good enough writer to make it, and pursuing a career in teaching was like accepting defeat before you'd started. Even so, the truth was that going back to school hadn't really been an option until he'd made it one. Suddenly I started thinking how wrong money was, what an evil system it was, how it poisoned people and could inspire them to betray themselves. I got very righteous and thought how much better it was to be poor, because money was like a gauze that went up around the person who had it and through which the world changed and became false. I thought how much more true life was without money, and how much better, therefore, for writing. Then I started thinking about Katherine, and how it would change everything between us just to mention what her father had said. What her father had said seemed toxic enough to

destroy something beautiful and fragile
about Katherine, something I couldn't quite
put my finger on. But in the next letter I
got from her she said that her father had
offered to send her on an extended trip
around Europe if she would only reconsider,
would only be willing to postpone the wedding. She said that he'd told her as well
what he'd offered me. She wanted to know what
I thought. After all, offers like that didn't
come along every day. And it wouldn't change
the way she felt about me. We had to be prac-
tical, she said. We had to be realistic. I
wrote back and told her that if she wanted
to take his money then she should. I told her
that if money was more important to her than
being with me then I had misjudged her, because it certainly wasn't more important to
me. I really let her have it. As soon as I sent
it I started regretting it. It wasn't fair at
all, because of course I had felt the same
way, that I couldn't just ignore an offer like
his. So right away I called her on the telephone and said that I'd written her a letter
in anger but that she should ignore it when
it arrived and the truth of the matter was
that her father's offer was driving a wedge
between us and that was the bottom line on
the whole thing. I made her see what a mali-
cious thing it was her father was doing, and
I even talked to her a little bit about how
money was a corrupting force and how it poisoned people, and by the end of the conversation I had her ready to tell her father off. I

told her that I would come up that weekend
and we could tell him our decision together,
and that there was nothing he could do
about it.

Hephaestus

One

From the station we took a taxi up to the hotel. The hotel was high up on the mountain, just above the town we had come to visit. A friend of Katherine's father had been there several years earlier, and had convinced him that it was the perfect place for us to go. On the drive Katherine put her head on my shoulder and tried to sleep. She hadn't slept all night, because the motion of the train had kept her awake. The taxi wasn't much better, though. I watched out the window, wondering how much snow was left now that the season was ending, and wondering too because they'd told me at the station when I'd asked that there had been no big snows for nearly a month. I knew that it didn't matter, because Katherine had asked me not to ski and I had promised her that I wouldn't. The son of a family down the block from her parents had been killed in a skiing accident, or something like that, and she was convinced that skiing was prohibitively dangerous. I'd always enjoyed skiing, and had been planning to go until she made me promise that I wouldn't. I didn't mind promising, so long as it made her happy. Even still, I couldn't keep myself from thinking about it. When we got to the hotel she asked me what I was thinking about, and because I didn't want to fight about it I told her I was thinking about what it must have been like to cross mountains before cars and airplanes and all of that. She'd seemed slightly annoyed with me the whole trip, and I didn't want to give her an excuse. I told myself that she was just tired, but of course she hadn't been tired when the trip began.

"Yes," she said absently, "that must have really been something." We looked together up the face of the slope, running behind the hotel. I watched the gondola coming up and the skiers coming down, and the bare places where the snowpack had melted through. "I'm so glad you gave up skiing," she said, yawning into her fist. "People get killed all the time. Even people with lots of experience."

"You're right," I said, still watching the skiers, hoping that if I agreed she would warm up to me.

The porter had come out and was unloading our bags. "But Miss," he said, setting the bags on the curb, "what will sir do, if not ski?"

"Sir will write," said my wife.

"Ah," said the porter, "sir is a writer?"

"Yes," Katherine said, "a very great American writer." I couldn't tell from her tone whether she was trying to build me up or laugh at me.

"Is this true," said the doorman, stopping what he was doing and turning to me, "that you are a great American writer?" And then, before I could respond, he said, "We had Roberto Ticholleti, the Italian filmmaker, last season. Do you know him? His picture is in the lobby. He is shaking hands with the concierge. We had two filmmakers, one singer, and three writers last season." He listed them off by counting on his fingers. "This season we will take a picture of you, the great American writer!" He laughed, excited by the celebrity he thought I was.

"I'm sorry," I said, "but my wife is having a joke on you. I'm not a famous writer. I'm a completely unfamous writer. My picture wouldn't be worth the frame you'd hang it in. We're here to ski, like everybody else."

"Then I hope for you that we get a big snow," he said, laughing to show that he didn't mind the joke Katherine had played on him.

"That's very nice of you," I said. "They told me at the station that you haven't had much this year."

"Not so much," said the porter, shaking his head.

"I'm going to see about the reservation," said Katherine, moving toward the door.

"Have you had much skiing yourself?" I asked, when she was gone.

"Oh no," said the porter, occupying himself with the bags, "not very much."

He turned again to unloading the bags and I watched him and tried to imagine how I would describe him if I were writing about him. I wished again that I was a famous writer, and I was anxious for the fame that I imagined was coming to me. If only something would sell. It only took one thing, because after that they knew that you could do it and would let you if you asked. That was all there was to it, I thought, as I overtipped the porter with Katherine's father's money. That was all there was to it, and after that nothing else would matter because I would be happy in ways that nothing else could touch. All of my failure and all of the ways that I had suffered would be worth it, I thought, though of course at that age I knew little of failure and even less of suffering. With what little I knew of them I had convinced myself that I knew something worth repeating. I watched the gondola rise and the skiers fall, thinking of how I would describe them. Then Katherine called to me sharply from the open door, and after a moment I went inside to find her and check into our room.

TWO

I found her leaning against the reception desk, talking to the clerks. They were a man and a woman clerk. The man was younger than the woman, but still older, I thought, than me. The man was handing the key to my wife.

"I've had my mail sent to the hotel," I said to the man.

"Of course," said the man. "Would you like it delivered to your room, or should we keep it at the desk?"

"Keep it here," I said. "I'd rather read it down here anyway."

The porter rode the elevator with us. He wheeled the baggage cart down the hall after us, refusing my help. We stood by the door and waited for him. Then one of the bags fell off the cart and I went back to help him despite his refusal. When I came back Katherine had the door open and was already inside. I went in after and the porter followed last. Outside the windows the mountainside rose away and showed blinding white in the afternoon sun. I crossed the room and stood staring out. Katherine took the phone and moving into the bathroom, saying "I promised daddy I'd telephone him the moment we arrived."

"All right," I said, "I'll unpack my things." The porter had unloaded our bags and I separated mine from hers, and then picked one of the bureaus and started unpacking. I could hear her in the other room, but I couldn't hear what she was saying. It made me nervous, although I told myself that I was being paranoid. I took all of the clothes, still folded, from the suitcases and put them, folded, into the drawers. I don't usually fold my clothes and wouldn't have folded them for the trip, I'm sure, if Katherine's parents' maid hadn't folded them for me. Looking at them, all folded in neat rows inside the drawers, I had the rather disconcerting impression that these weren't my clothes, but belonged to someone else.

Katherine came out, holding the telephone in its cradle. I slipped off my shoes and climbed up onto the bed on my knees. She did the same and as she came forward into my arms I slid to my side and she moved over me. I felt her warm breath on my face and then her mouth over mine, and the gentle ridges of her teeth were against my lips, and for a moment I had the warm and idiotic sense that she was mine in some eternal way, that she would be mine forever. Then that feeling vanished, because without meaning to I had begun to wonder how many other men had kissed her lips and felt this same. I tried hard to remember that this didn't matter, and that I had kissed other girls before, and that those didn't mean that I was any less hers now than she was mine. Still, I wondered if it was the same.

"What did your father have to say?" I asked, breaking away.

"Nothing much," she said. "We talked about where we would live when you worked at the company."

"And what did you decide?"

"Well," she said, folding her hands on my chest and resting her chin on them, "daddy said that when we get back he'll help us look for something. Something nearby."

"We can't afford something nearby."

"Daddy said not to worry about all of that. He said that he'd take care of whatever we couldn't." She rested her head on my chest, and I smoothed her hair down her back. Then she rolled off the bed and crossed the room to the window. I followed her and wrapped my arms around her waist. "Isn't it wonderful here?" she said, looking out at the slope. I kissed the side of her neck and then down along the line of her shoulder and across her throat as she turned. "I have to unpack and change," she said. "We have reservations for dinner in less than an hour."

"Where?" I said, holding her hips and guiding her back towards me.

"Here," she said, pulling against my hands. "The restaurant in the hotel."

"Then they can wait."

"Daddy called and made the reservations," she said, "and he said to be on time. Don't get sulky. There's plenty of time for that later."

"I'm not being sulky," I said, "this is my normal face." She didn't say anything to that. She had already crossed the room and was beginning to unpack her suitcases. "All right," I said, "I'm going down the bar. Come down when you're finished.

Three

I left the room and went down the hall.
When I came around the corner I caught sight
of my reflection in the elevator doors, and
for a moment everything stopped making
sense. I had the thought that I was looking
at Katherine's husband, but that somehow
made the reflection seem like it wasn't me.
Then the doors slid open and I stepped inside, and without the reflection there I felt
like myself again.

Downstairs the bar was crowded, and I had
to push between people to get to the bartender. I ordered gin and tonic and squeezed
the lime in myself when he brought it. Then I
faced out from the bar and looked around,
thinking that I might use the bar as the
setting for a story. The bar was fairly
crowded. At the table in front of me a man in
a military uniform I didn't recognize was
standing beside a seated group of men and
women. The women were all watching the man
in the uniform, and the men at the table were
all watching the women. Every time the man
in the uniform would say something the

women would laugh and the men would drink.
The woman sitting closest to him, in the outside seat of the booth, put her hand on the
soldier's arm, and the man across from her
took another drink and looked up into the
ceiling. The soldier kissed the woman's hand.
Then all of a sudden my drink was almost
finished and so I turned back to the bar,
thinking that I would order another and if
Katherine came then I could take it with me
into the restaurant. I hadn't thought that
the altitude would affect me, but I was already feeling warm and a little lightheaded. I waved the bartender down as he
passed and ordered another gin and tonic,
and asked him if this time he would please
put in some gin. He nodded and began to mix
the drink. Then the man next to me called to
the bartender, and the bartender leaned in
and said something that I didn't understand.

"No, no," said the man next to me. He
pointed to the man on the other side of him.
The man on the other side was young, with a
sunburned face and white rings around his
eyes. The bartender turned to the man and
the man nodded, and the bartender came up
with the bottle of wine and filled the man's
glass. He glanced up at me as though he expected me to be upset that he had filled the
man's glass while I was waiting for my drink.
When I didn't say anything he finished and
came back with my drink. I took it and
thanked him and he moved away again.

I faced out from the bar and watched the
soldier cross the room with one of the girls
from the table on his arm. The others from
the table were behind them and the man who
was left alone followed last, scowling at the
soldier's back and tucking his billfold into
his pocket. I was feeling very lightheaded
and so I turned back and hunched over my
drink, wondering where Katherine was.

Then, someone tapped me on the shoulder.

"Are you American?" said the owner of the
hand that had tapped me. It was the young
man with the white rings around his eyes. He
had come around to my side of the other man.
He was swaying slightly and his face was
angry.

"Yes," I said, "is there a problem?"

A slow smile crossed the young man's face
and creased it where the tanned skin was
stiff across his cheeks. He stuck out a hand.
"Not at all," he said, shaking my hand, "just
glad to meet someone else who understands
me. Been trying to get this jackass to understand me all day." He pointed over my shoulder at the other man, who was drinking his
wine and paying no attention. "You here for
the skiing?"

"No," I said, "I'm on my honeymoon."

"Oh," he said. "Well, congratulations then."

"Thank you," I said.

"I was just going to say," he went on, "that
if you are going to go skiing, don't hire that
one to guide you." He was talking loud
enough for the other man to hear.

"He's no good?"

"No good at all."

"Then why did you hire him?" I asked

"They told me in town that he was the best," he said, not embarrassed. "I think he's a bit of a village idiot. I think they pawn him off on the tourists. Lousy deceitful bastards. They think all Americans are rich and can afford to pay for a whole day of no skiing and not feel cheated."

He was looking at the man over his shoulder, and I looked with him. The man had finished the wine in his glass and was calling the bartender over. The bartender came and the man said something that I didn't understand, and the bartender turned and looked at the American. The American shook his head and the bartender turned back to the guide to tell him, but the guide shook his head and, as we watched, drew several bills from his pocket and handed them over. He was either drunk or didn't care to begin with. The bartender filled the glass again. The guide took it happily.

"Bastard," said the other American, shaking his head. "I've been buying his drinks all damn afternoon."

"You didn't go up at all?"

"We went up for a bit. The bastard said the snow pack was unstable. That wasn't even the word he used. He said the snow pack was irresolute, if you've ever heard of such a thing."

"Maybe he's right."

"Maybe he knew I'd buy his drinks." He didn't say anything for a while. Then he said, "Are you staying in the hotel?"

"Yes. Are you?"

"Yes. Three more nights. Maybe I'll see you back here again. Fancy that at this point I'd be happy to buy a drink for someone I can understand."

"Good," I said, shaking his hand. And then I said, "Hope you have better luck skiing tomorrow."

"Thanks," he said. "And congratulations again."

"Oh, yes," I said. "I'd forgotten that we were talking about it."

Four

After the other American left, the bar was almost empty. Everyone else had gone to dinner, I guessed. Then the bartender looked up and waved someone over. I turned and saw a tall man coming across the room. He leaned against the bar on the other side of the American's guide and started talking to him. I couldn't understand what he was saying.

"No, no," the guide kept saying, "one more. One more, then I go." The other man kept talking the whole time. After a while the guide stopped talking and nodded and stood up. The new man stood with him and held him gently by the arm. The bartender said something and the new man pulled a bill from his pocket and handed it across. The bartender seemed satisfied. The new man took the guide out into the lobby, and I stopped watching them and wondered where Katherine was.

Then the new man came back and sat down next to me. The bartender came over and the new man ordered a drink. Then he bought me a drink. He thought I was the American that had hired the guide. I explained to him that

I wasn't, that I had just arrived. The new man told the bartender to bring me a drink anyway. He asked me if I planned to ski and I explained that my wife had made me promise that I wouldn't.

"Ah," said the new man, "a wife can be a tricky thing."

"I'm starting to figure that out," I said.

"If you don't mind me asking," he said, "how old are you?"

"I'm twenty-two," I said.

"That is the right age to figure it out," he said. Neither of us said anything for a while. Then the new man said, a little incredulously, "What do you plan to do, if you don't plan to ski?"

"We're going to see the town," I said. "My father-in-law had a friend who came here. He said the town was wonderful. And I'm going to try to write."

"Oh," he said, "what do you write?"

"I write stories," I said. "I wrote a novel, too."

"Anything I would have read?"

"They haven't been published over here," I said, thinking that this was a clever way to answer the question.

"What is your name?" he said. "So I can ask about your book if I am ever in America."

"James Smith," I said, feeling foolish for having tried to bluff him.

"Thomas Orestes," he said, and we shook hands. "Maybe, if you decide to write something about the town, you could ask me what-

ever you want to know. I've lived here my entire life. I know everything there is to know
about it."

"Sure," I said, "I'll keep that in mind."

"Maybe you'll even decide that you want to
write about me," he said, and laughed to show
that he was only joking.

"That depends," I said, going along with
him. "What do you do?"

"I'm a guide," he said, "up on the mountain."

"That does sound very interesting," I said.
"What does a day in the life of a ski guide
consist of?" I was a little drunk and feeling
playful now that the fear that he would dis-
cover that I wasn't much of a writer at all,
and had nothing published, had passed.

"Oh, it's very interesting," he said. "It
would make a terrific story. Every morning
we meet at the lodge. Then the head guide
tells us which of us has been hired and
which of us has not. Then everyone who has
been hired gets into a van and goes up to
the lift to meet their clients. Then we ski.
Then we get paid. Then we go home. Then we do
it over again." He laughed again to show
that he knew that this did not sound very
interesting, and that he had been joking
when he'd said that it was.

"I've never written about anything like
that," I said.

"One time one of the clients fell from the
lift," he said. "They thought that one of the
guides had pushed him. You could write about
that."

"I don't write mysteries," I said. I looked
at my watch. It had been almost an hour
since I'd left her. I wondered if she was
looking for me, and what I should do about
it. I'd told her I was going to the bar. and I
thought that if she was looking for me she
would know where to look, and I thought that
even if she assumed I'd gone to the restaurant to claim the reservation she would come
back to the bar when she realized that I
wasn't there. The whole thing was making me,
for some reason, very nervous. I had the
rather ridiculous and admittedly drunken
notion that she'd gone off somewhere without
me, and left me behind. But just as I was
thinking that, she came in. She came over
when she saw me and stood with her arms
crossed, tapping her foot. For some reason it
was a bit embarrassing to see her do it.

"Well," she said, "you certainly made yourself hard to find."

"I said that I would be in the bar," I said.
And then I said, "I'd like you to know Thomas
Orestes. Thomas, this is my wife Katherine."

"It is very nice to meet you," he said,
standing from his stool and shaking her
hand.

"Thomas is a guide on the mountain," I
said. I have no idea why I said it.

"A ski guide," Katherine said with mock
wonder, looking at me. "James, why ever have
you been talking to a ski guide?"

"We were talking about writing," Thomas
said.

"Oh, of course," said Katherine, with the same tone of mock wonder. "But oh my goodness, you'll have to excuse us. We are fantastically late for our dinner reservation."

"Of course," Thomas said.

"Will you be around?" I asked, as Katherine took my hand and began dragging me from the bar. "I mean, if I decide that I want to write about you?" It was my attempt to respond to his jokes with a joke, but it just sounded superior when I said it. Even so, he didn't seem to mind.

"Yes," he said, "come find me at the lodge. The bartender knows where it is."

"Terrific," I said. "I'll buy you a drink."

"All right," he said, "but only if you will let me read something you've written."

"Certainly," I said, "it's a deal."

Then we were out of the bar, and our steps were loud on the lobby's marble floor. I walked staring at my feet, watching them closely because they wouldn't do quite what I wanted them to do. They dragged and kicked in a terribly obvious and embarrassing way. I glanced back and saw that Thomas was over at the bar, and was paying for our drinks. I made a note to buy all of the drinks next time, but was sure that I would forget.

"Katherine," I said, "help me remember to buy Thomas a drink."

"Oh please," she said, dragging me, "you're not buying that man anything. These people are vultures. Now pick up your feet, please. We're late enough already."

Five

The headwaiter led us to a booth near the back of the room. Katherine asked for something, I didn't hear what, and I put my head against the seat back and closed my eyes. I could feel Katherine's annoyance but I was feeling drunk enough to tell myself that I didn't care.

Then Katherine started talking. I don't remember what she said. Watching her speak I realized how drunk I was by the way that my thoughts wouldn't stay put. I was thinking about what I was going to say to her when she was finished, but once I had found the words and moved from one point to the next the first point disappeared, and in the meantime I'd missed what she'd said, and I couldn't remember what I was going to say. I remember her saying that she wasn't going to spend her honeymoon trying to prove to me that she was well-read enough or smart enough to be my wife, and only remember that because it surprised me so much that I stopped thinking about what I was going to say to her and wondered instead if I really had tried to make her feel that way. I decided that I hadn't, because I'd only ever given her a few books that I thought she should have read, and hadn't said anything about it when she'd stopped reading them, and even that had been a long time ago, before we were even dating. Then I tried to pay attention, because while I had been thinking that she'd said a lot of other things.

Suddenly, thinking about giving her books to read, and that time in our lives, I felt that I didn't want to fight with her now or ever again. I just wanted everything to be all right between us. So I interrupted her and started telling her why I'd wanted her to read the books that I'd given her, about how they captured something about me that I wanted her to understand, and with other books about how they had given me so much pleasure or had changed me, and I'd wanted her to experience that. Then I started talking about the day I'd realized I wanted to marry her, the day when she'd told me that when she was young she'd imagined that there was a house under the sea where she could hide from everything in the world that made her afraid. Then I tried to explain how I wanted to be that for her, wanted to be for her what she'd imagined she'd have in a house under the sea, and when I said that she brought her fist down on the seat cushion beside her and told me in a low, hard voice that I wasn't allowed to speak of that or especially write about that, not ever.

I remember being surprised, but I
shouldn't have been. I should have known how
she would take it. I knew her well enough to
know that it would drive her crazy, someone
knowing something like that about her, even
me. I was going to say something else, but
right then the waiter came back and so I
opened my menu and pretended that I was
reading it. I could feel my cheeks burning,
and because I was drunk I was having a hard
time thinking about anything else. Then the
waiter went away and I realized that Katherine had ordered for me. I leaned my head
back and closed my eyes again. All of a sudden I was feeling very tired.

We sat there for a long time, neither of us
saying anything. Then I couldn't stand it
anymore, and so I said, "Katherine, please
don't be angry." I didn't have the energy to
try to convince her. I just wanted her to
stop.

"I'm not angry," she said.

"Don't be upset, then. Or tell me what it is.
You've been annoyed with me this whole time."

"I'm not upset." she said. "I don't know what
you're talking about."

"Please," I said. "Don't be difficult."

"All right," she said, looking right at me,
"I won't be difficult. I'll be however you want
me to be. How's that?"

But I didn't say anything to that, because
right then the damn waiter brought our sal-
ads. When he left she said, before I could say
anything, "All right, I'll tell you something.

I'll give you something you can use for one
of your little stories. I've got something
that would make a terrific short story. Do
you want to hear it? When I was sixteen I
was going with a boy named Charlie Fitch.
Charlie and I used to go out every weekend.
We'd drive out somewhere in Charlie's father's
car. I always told my parents that we were
going to the movies but we never did. Charlie's best friend was a guy named Gene and
Gene was going with a girl named Diedra. A
lot of times we'd go out together. We'd drink
whatever one of us was able to get from our
parents' bar. Gene and Diedra would be in the
front seat, and Charlie and I would be in the
back. Or sometimes it was the other way
around. Gene was a terrifically good-looking
guy. The best-looking guy in school, by far.
So one night Charlie and I go to pick up
Gene and he tells us that he's not coming
out, that Diedra broke it off with him, that
she's fallen in love with someone else. Well I
just feel terrible for Gene, because he's obviously really broken up about it. Charlie
says that Gene should come out with us anyway, that it'll be good for him to get out, and
that it's no good for him to mope around his
parents' house. So Gene gets in and he starts
saying a lot of things about how Diedra is
right to break it off, how he's no good and
all that. We drive around with him talking
like that for a while, and then we park
somewhere out in the middle of nowhere. We're
all drinking from this bottle of scotch that

Gene brought. I remember thinking how upset
he must be to bring the whole bottle, because
his parents were going to notice that it was
missing. Usually we just filled a flask.
Charlie and I are both trying to convince
Gene that it doesn't matter about Diedra, that
a lot of great girls would be more than
happy to go with him. Then Charlie says, I
bet Katherine would go with you in a heart-
beat, wouldn't you Katherine? And of course I
say of course. And Charlie says, and I
wouldn't mind, either. And Gene looks at me
with this kind of desperate, hurting look on
his face and says, is that true? Like my answer means absolutely everything to him. And
I say of course it's true because it is true,
because I would. And to show him that I mean
it I lean over the seat and I kiss him. And I
don't stop kissing him. And then I go over
into the back with Gene. And Charlie wasn't
kidding. He didn't mind at all. He watched the
whole thing."

After she said that she didn't say
anything else. I couldn't think of anything
to say. After a while, just to break the silence, I said, "Jesus, Katherine." And then, because I couldn't think of anything else to
say after that, I said, "Jesus Christ. Why the
hell would you tell me something like that?"

"You wanted to talk about me when I was
young," she said, her face the picture of in-
nocence. "I'm sorry, did I misunderstand you?
Didn't you want to talk about me when I was
young? I thought I was doing what you

wanted me to do. And anyways you're a writer. I thought you could use it."

After that we didn't talk anymore. The waiter brought our food, but I didn't eat anything. I kept drinking the wine Katherine had ordered until the bottle was gone. Then a while later the waiter came back and asked if we would like desert, and Katherine told him no. Then she took my arm and led me out of the restaurant and across the empty lobby. I watched the desk clerk as I stumbled past and he didn't look up. I imagined that I was making a scene, and that he was not looking out of respect for my dignity. I wanted to do something to show him that I appreciated it, that I was drunk but that I wasn't an obnoxious drunk American like the others, that I had some class. I thought that I could tip him and tell him what a great job he was doing. I asked Katherine to stop but she wouldn't, and I watched the desk clerk as he moved farther and farther away behind us, and I thought that maybe the classiest thing to do would be to leave him alone.

Six

We got on the elevator and rode up, and when the doors opened I got out quickly and walked down the hall ahead of her. As I neared the door I felt inside my pockets and couldn't find the key. I had to wait for her. She had the key out and I tried to take it from her but she held it out of my reach. I closed my eyes and leaned against the wall. Then we were inside and through the window I could see the line of lights from the gondola winding up the dark mountain. I went over to the window and leaned against the glass, feeling it cool my palm and then my forehead. Then Katherine's arms were around me, and I could feel her breath against my neck. I stayed staring out for a moment, letting the window hold me in place before I turned into her, and we crossed the room to the bed.

I don't remember most of what happened next. I remember that the look on her face scared me because it was a look that said something was wrong, though it was the face she always made and I had seen it before. Then I remember knowing that it had come and gone and that I didn't remember what it had been like. Then sleep was coming on irresistibly, and I turned away from her and watched the lights winding up the mountain until I fell asleep.

When I woke it was morning and my head was throbbing. Katherine wasn't in the bed but I could hear the shower running. I wanted very badly to fall back asleep. I lay with my eyes closed and pretended that I wasn't awake. After a while the shower stopped and Katherine came out and got back into bed with me.

"Good morning," she said.

"Morning," I said, rolling to meet her and feeling the sheets damp from her underneath my shoulder, "how did you sleep?"

"I slept well. How did you sleep?"

"I slept very well."

"Would you like some breakfast? I can call down for some."

"Have you already had yours?"

"No. I waited for you."

She rolled away from me and sat up, and I reached out and ran my fingers

along the bumps of her spine. I closed my
eyes and listened to her talking to the
desk clerk and felt her moving slightly
under my fingers. After a moment she
said, "They already stopped serving
breakfast. They say they can send lunch."
I nodded without opening my eyes and
listened as she finished the order and
hung up. When she was finished she went
back into the bathroom. I lay for a while,
listening to the muffled sound of her
moving around through the wall. Then
there was a knock at the door, and I got
out of bed and went to see about it. While
I was putting on my pants there was another knock, and I called that I was coming, and the sound of my own raised voice
made my head hurt even more. I opened the
door and the room service waiter came in,
pulling the cart in after him.

"I'll leave cart," he said. "House keeping will pick it up later. All right?"

"Yes," I said, looking for my wallet to
tip him.

"Is there anything else?" He was waiting next to the door.

"No," I said, feeling through my pockets and finally finding my wallet. And
then, so that there wouldn't be a long si-
lent pause in which it became awkward
about him waiting for the money, I said,

"Are there good places to eat in town?" I
had the money out, now, and handed it to
him.

"Oh yes," he said, taking the bills
without looking at them. "There are a lot
of good restaurants in the town." He
listed off several, and what they were
known for, and what they looked like so I
would be able to recognize them, and
where they were. Several of them were lo-
cated around the square, he said, and
when the weather was nice the restaurants would all line the square with tables. He said that the town was really
rather famous for it. It was something
that people came to see: all of the waiters, wearing the uniforms of the different restaurants, moving around each
other.

"Don't they get confused?" I asked.

"I've never heard of it," he said. "Is
there anything else?"

I told him there was nothing else. He
left and I closed the door behind him. I
looked at the food and I waited for Katherine. Then, when a long time had passed
and she still hadn't come out, I decided
that she probably wouldn't mind, and so I
ate. While I was eating I remembered the
story she'd told at dinner, about her and
the good-looking heartbroken kid in the

backseat of her boyfriend's car. I hadn't remembered it right away when I woke up. Remembering it was like hearing it all over again. I told myself that it was a long time ago and that it didn't matter anyway. That didn't make me feel any better about it, though. The story was one thing, and her telling it to me was something else.

She came out and lay back on the mattress. I lay back too and rested my head lightly on her shoulder. I could feel her heart beating against my cheek.

"What are you thinking about?" I asked, after we'd been like that for a while.

"I was thinking about what we're going to do today. What do you want to do?"

"I was thinking that I might try to write something," I said. "I'd like to try to get something written while we're here. I've got some ideas that I've been working out. I'd like to see if I can get them down." I nuzzled into her shoulder. She didn't move at all. "But I really don't care," I said. "I can do that later. I can do that when we get back. What did you want to do today?"

"I was reading about the town in the guide my parents gave us," she said. "Did you know that you can take a horse-drawn carriage ride up the mountain? Not all the way to the top, but a long way up one of the trails. It's supposed to be just beautiful. You hire one out in the square and they take you around town and then up this road into the trees. You stop at a clearing and can look out over the whole town."

"All right," I said, "what else?"

"There's a lot to see," she said. "The guidebook says that the plaza has a fountain that was cast from bronze mined from the mountain. It said that the fountain is fed from a spring up on the mountainside, and that the water is piped down the mountain and then up into a tank inside one of the buildings. It says that the height of the fountain can be adjusted by a valve on the bottom of the tank. It says that there's a blacksmith in the old part of town, the part they keep old-fashioned for the tourists, and that once every twenty-five years he has to replace all of the rivets inside of the fountain and in the pipes leading down to it from the tank. It said that once a century the blacksmith has had to re-place all of the rivets along the whole stretch of pipe, from the spring down to the town."

"I wonder why they don't just replace it with something else," I said. "Something that won't rust."

"I don't know," she said. "The guidebook says that the whole town comes out and works on it. Everything stops for a month, and everybody works on it together."

"What else is there?"

"There are a lot of things. What do you want to see?"

"I don't know," I said. "I don't care." I was thinking about it again, even though I was trying not to.

Seven

We got dressed and went downstairs. Katherine asked the desk clerk about renting a carriage, and he said that we should talk to the bartender at one of the restaurants in town. The bartender ran the schedule, the clerk said, and the bar was where the coachmen went between tours. While they were talking I leaned back against the desk and watched the people milling around the lobby. There were several couples, and a few men who looked like they were there to ski and hadn't brought their wives. Most of them were going into or coming out of the restaurant. Then I watched a woman get out of the elevator alone and cross the lobby. When she walked past us she looked back at me and I looked away, embarrassed that I had been watching her so obviously. Then Katherine tapped me on the shoulder and right away I felt very tired again and thought that it was just as well that I hadn't stayed in the room and tried to write, because I would have either fallen asleep or written badly and had to start over again anyway.

"He says that the carriages go out all the time during the season," she said, "but that now that the season is over there are not as many running and we'll have to talk to the bartender and see if there are any coachmen to take us."

"All right," I said, looking back at the woman who was now passing through the lobby doors. "Did he tell you where to go?"

"He gave me the name of the place. He said it's easy to find."

"All right."

We went out into the bright sunshine and my head hurt twice as much. Katherine took my hand, and we went together down the hill towards town. The incline was very steep. Looking down you could see over the buildings to the far side of the square. We descended quickly and then we were in among the buildings.

We found the restaurant that the clerk had named. Inside it was dim and I was glad, because the sunlight was making my eyes hurt. We sat down at the bar and the bartender came over. Katherine asked him about a carriage ride and he explained that since it was the off season the carriage had not been prepared, and the horses were not bridled. He said that if we did not mind waiting everything could be arranged, and we could still have one.

"That's fine," said Katherine. "We don't mind waiting."

We ordered beer and the bartender brought
them. We drank and waited. The beer was cold
and drinking it I felt better. I was grateful
for the bar and for the fact that we could
get in out of the sun. I sat thinking about
nothing and letting myself think about
nothing. Then there was a lot of noise outside, and the door opened and four men came
in. The soldier from the bar was with them.
He stood in the front, still in his uniform,
and when I turned to say something to Katherine about it I saw that she was already
looking at him. The four sat down at a table
in the back, and a while after that the door
opened and another man came alone. He
looked at the bartender, who pointed to us.

"You wanted a carriage?" the man called to
me.

"Yes," said Katherine, getting down off the
stool. I paid for our drinks and followed
them outside. The carriage was drawn up in
front of the bar. The driver crossed in front
of the horses and climbed up into his seat.
Katherine climbed up into the carriage and I
followed her. When we were up the driver
snapped the reigns and the carriage started
off. We passed through a side street and then
around a corner into the square. In the middle of the square stood the fountain. It was
perhaps thirty feet high, and very impres-
sive. The base rose in layers and made a
platform at twenty or so feet on which a man
was sitting. The man's legs were curled awkwardly beneath him and he leaned on one arm

while the other reached upward. His bearded
face was turned up as well. There were girls
sitting beside him and at his feet. One had
her arms around him, holding him up. The
others looked with pity at his ruined legs.

"Who is that?" I said, yelling slightly
over the clatter of the hooves.

"Who?" said the driver.

"The fountain," I yelled. "Who is that on
the fountain?"

"That is Hephaestus," he said without
looking at it.

We rode on through the square and then
turned off again, heading up the mountain. I
leaned back into the seat and put my arm
around Katherine. She leaned into me and I
was happy. The wheels clattered against the
pavement and the carriage swung from side
to side. Then the incline grew steeper and I
glanced back and watched the buildings fall
away and I saw the long rows of shingled
roofs and chimneys and beyond, the sparkle
of sunlight that I imagined was off the water from the fountain.

We rode along on a road held in close by
the forest. Away to our right and through a
break in the trees I saw the hotel and the
road leading to it, and above it the gondola.
We crossed a river and a saw a rusted pipe
running alongside the bank and under the
bridge. I pointed it out to Katherine.

"That must be the pipe from the spring," I
said, "the one they use to run the fountain."
I could see the roof of the hotel now, and

the skiers moving down the run below us. The
road beyond the bridge was narrower and
rougher and the horses' hooves crunched
against the grit and the carriage wheels
creaked and slid.

"Jimmy," said Katherine, "tell him to go
back. Tell him to turn around."

"All right."

"Please," she said.

I leaned forward with difficulty against
the incline and tapped the driver on the
shoulder.

"Thank you all the same," I said, "but I
think my wife would like to go back to town
now."

"It's not too far," he said, without turning
around. I felt the wheels of the carriage begin to go and then catch and I heard Katherine gasp slightly behind me.

"Really," I said, "I appreciate that. We'll
pay for the whole trip. It's just that my wife
is really more in the mood to look around
town." The wheels slid again, and the nervous
sounds of the horses carried over their
backs to us. "Please," I said.

"Not now," he said. "The road is too narrow.
I cannot turn the horses."

"What did he say?" Katherine said, when I
fell back against the seat.

"He said that he can't turn around here,
because the road is too narrow."

"Tell him he has to," she said. "Tell him he
has to turn around."

"He can't," I said.

Ahead of us the road cut away and trav-
ersed along a ledge beneath which a cliff
split the mountainside in a vertical gray
slab. As we came around onto it I felt the
wheels begin to slide and then catch and
then slide again. Then we came around and
the carriage rolled onto the shelf and I
could see the town far below us. The driver
pulled in the reins and the horses stopped.
The mountain stretched away below us, broken
first by the stony gash of the cliff and
then, farther below, by a stand of trees, with
the road winding in and out of sight among
the branches. Then the road ran clear along
the exposed mountainside, growing smaller in
the distance, switching back across the open
stretches of grass and snow where the trees
had been cleared away, and the first of the
houses began, short and squat and green-
roofed. Beyond was the village and the
square and the fountain, still visible, and
then more buildings and houses stretching
farther down as the mountain rose up on either side and fell away into a valley between, with the road running down and then
arching up to cross the ridges as it fell.
Then, far below, the dots of buildings and
the lines of the railroad, cutting across the
open valley, and the land squared off in
farm lots and dense and black around the
city beyond the tracks. Then, still farther
out, green hills and white mountains, dappled in places by the shadows of clouds.

"Write this," Katherine said, pressing herself against me. "Oh my God, Jim. Write this just like it is."

"I will," I said, feeling the happiest I'd been since the trip began. "Someday when I'm good enough I will."

Eight

We stayed for a long time, looking out at the town and the valley below and the mountains beyond. I could see the train blowing a trail of white across the valley floor and I remembered the mail and reminded myself to ask the clerk when we returned. Thinking about it I began to get impatient to go back and I reminded myself that most likely nothing had come, and that I should stay as long as Katherine wanted to and as long as she was happy and enjoy it.

"Will you write about us, too?" she said after a while. "Will you write about how happy we were, when we stood here together?"

"I'll try to," I said. "It's a hard thing to write about."

"You can do it," she said, hugging my arm. "I know you can do it."

"It's not that I can't do it," I said, a little annoyed at her talking like she knew anything about it, and annoyed too that now she was happy and acting like she had not been difficult for nearly two days. "It's hard to write about it and make it interesting to other people. Nobody wants to read about two people who are happy. People like stories much better where everyone is unhappy and nothing works out. Other people's happiness is boring to read about."

"That's silly," she said. "When people read what you write about us being happy they should be happy for us. They should be happy that we're happy."

"They won't be," I said. "They'll be bored to tears."

Then we didn't say anything for a while, and I felt sorry for being annoyed with her. I reminded myself that it wasn't her fault that she didn't know anything about it and besides, she had been trying to say something nice. But just thinking about her saying it I got annoyed all over again. I thought that I would write what I damn well pleased, and that she didn't have anything to say about it.

We stood for a while longer, and then Katherine asked if I was hungry and if I wanted to go back down. She hadn't eaten the lunch that she'd ordered at the hotel. I told her I would go whenever she was ready and she said that she was ready now. I told the driver, and he climbed up into the seat and took the reins. He took the coach across the shelf to a clearing on the other side and turned it, and we started down. We moved seats and sat facing uphill, with everything moving away from us. After a while this made

me nauseous and so I closed my eyes and
tried not to think about anything.

The square was crowded and I paid the
driver while Katherine went to look for a
table. As she walked away she looked in all
the shop windows and it suddenly made me
very happy because I knew that she would do
it and it seemed to me that I knew her very
well. I was happy because I thought that it
meant something. I leaned back against the
wall and watched the people moving around
the square. After a while Katherine came
back and said, "There aren't any tables. One
of the waiters told me that we'd have better
luck in an hour. I thought we were going to
miss the crowds, coming later in the season."

"These people don't look like tourists," I
said. "I think these people live here."

"Well, what do you want to do?" she said.
"Have a drink?"

"I'd like to run back to the hotel," I said.
"The train came in when we were up on the
carriage, and I want to see if any mail has
come for me. And I want to change my shirt.
It's too warm in this one."

"I'd like to take a look in some of these
shops," she said. "Maybe we should meet back
here in an hour or so? What do you think?"

"That sounds fine," I said. "If I don't take
that long I'll just come find you."

She kissed me on the cheek and I left the
square and walked back uphill towards the
hotel. It was a long walk, and hot in the sun,
and when I arrived there wasn't any mail. I

had sweated through my shirt and so I went up to the room and took a shower. I had plenty of time. While I was showering I starting thinking again about the story Katherine had told me. I had been thinking about it ever since I'd remembered it that morning, really, but now that she wasn't there to talk to and I didn't have the mail to wonder about I didn't have anything to keep me from thinking about it. I made myself think instead about how she had told that when she was young she had imagined that there was a house under the sea, where she could go and be safe. I don't know why, but right then I got an idea for a story that I could use it in. Her telling me not to use it or write about it made it somehow seem like the only thing I'd ever wanted to write about. I got out of the shower and wrote the outline of the idea down. When I had it down I finished my shower. Then I put on a fresh shirt, feeling excited in the way I always got when I had an idea started, and not thinking about Katherine's story anymore.

Nine

When I got to the square I couldn't see
Katherine, and spent twenty minutes looking
for her. Finally, I spotted her. She was
standing with her back to me, talking to the
soldier I had seen in the bar. The soldier
pointed toward me and Katherine turned and,
smiling, began to move through the crowd,
with the soldier weaving through behind her.

"Hello, darling," she said, putting her
arms around my neck. "Have you been waiting
long? I hope you haven't been waiting too
long. Have you had a drink? Neither have we.
Let's get one, shall we? Jim, this is Lieutenant Larkos. Lieutenant, this is my husband,
Jim."

"It's a pleasure to meet you," I said, putting out my hand.

"Likewise," he said, shaking my hand.

"Have a drink?"

"My pleasure," he said.

The square had cleared out a little, and
we found an empty table and sat down. A
waiter from one of the restaurants came over
but the Lieutenant waved him away and ges-

tured to one from another restaurant. The second one came and Katherine ordered our drinks.

"So," said the Lieutenant, "Katherine tells me that you are a writer."

"You were gone so long that I joked to the Lieutenant that you were writing another book," she explained. "Wasn't that clever of me?"

"Yes," I said, "that was very clever."

"You wrote a book, then?" the Lieutenant said.

"Yes," I said, "but only a small one."

"Well," he said, "may I read it?"

"Jimmy won't let anyone read it," Katherine said. "He won't even let me read it. He thinks I'm not smart enough to appreciate it." She said it in the light, indifferent tone she used when socializing with strangers.

"I never said that," I said.

"I know," she said in the same tone, "it's just your baby and you don't want to share it."

"It's not that I don't want to share it," I said, knowing even while I was speaking that I sounded too annoyed for the company and for the frivolous way in which she spoke. "It's just that I want to get it right before anyone reads it." The waiter had brought our drinks while we were talking and I took mine and drank, hoping that when I was finished the bad feeling and the bad taste of Katherine talking about the book would be gone.

"Don't you just love this town, Lieutenant?" Katherine said. "I just love this town."

"Oh yes," he said. "You have wonderful taste, for an American." He said it as a joke and they both laughed. "But Jim," he said, "and I hope I am not being impolite: what is your book about? Only if you don't mind me asking."

"It's boring," I said, drinking, "and besides, it's not finished."

"It is too finished," said Katherine. "And I'm sure it's not boring at all."

"Please," said the Lieutenant. "I am very interested, and promise not to be bored."

"All right," I said. I had the sense, suddenly, that lunch was going to take a very long time, and I wished that Katherine hadn't found the Lieutenant, and that we were eating alone together, and that I didn't have to talk about the book. At that time I thought that it was bad luck to talk about it like it was something before it had come to anything. But then I started telling them about it, and kept talking and talking. After a while I noticed that Katherine was sulking, and so I finished up. The waiter had brought our second round and I took a long drink of mine, feeling the way I had felt reading stories to people at school, feeling proud and indifferent, feeling like an artist among philistines, before I remembered that I was someone's husband, now, and that I was no longer allowed to feel that way.

"Well it sounds like a very good book," said the Lieutenant. "I would very much like to read it."

"Thank you," I said. "If the publisher accepts it I'll send you a copy."

"Is it getting published?"

"I'm waiting to hear."

"Good luck, then," he said.

"That was wonderful," said Katherine, coming suddenly and falsely out of her sulk. "Don't you think that was wonderful, Lieutenant? The way he described it, and all? And the story and the details, didn't you think it was all wonderful? I thought it was. You know, if you can believe it, I hadn't heard even that much about it. Isn't that strange? Jimmy hasn't told me even that much. I'm very excited about this story, Jimmy, I am. Jimmy is a very talented writer, you know. Very talented, and gifted, and everything he writes is very important and must be kept very secret or else it will be spoiled, isn't that right, Jim darling? Did you know that, Lieutenant? Would you have guessed? No, of course you wouldn't have. But it does sound like a wonderful book, doesn't it? It sounds just wonderful to me, Jim."

"Katherine," I said. "Please. It doesn't matter."

"No, it doesn't matter," she said. "Lieutenant, would you join us for lunch? I think I starved half to death, listening to Jim describe his book." She laughed and nobody laughed with her. "Do stay and eat with us," she said. "It's been nothing but the two of us since we started this trip. I'm dying for for some variety."

"I'll come only if Jim doesn't mind," said the Lieutenant.

"I don't mind," I said. "Of course I don't mind."

"Lovely," said Katherine.

We finished our drinks, and the Lieutenant suggested that we order from another restaurant. The waiter brought the bill for our drinks and the Lieutenant paid. Katherine insisted that she be allowed to, but the Lieutenant paid anyway.

"You might have let me offer to pay," I said quietly to her as the Lieutenant was flagging down another of the waiters.

"It's all my money anyway," she said quickly. And then she said, "anyway, I only said it to be polite. He insisted."

"Look," I said, "I'm sorry that I never told you anything about the book. I didn't know you thought anything of it. I didn't know you cared anything about it. You've never asked to read it."

"You asked me not to ask," she said.

A waiter had come over and the Lieutenant was ordering for us. Then he explained everything and asked if it sounded all right. We told him that it sounded fine and the waiter went away.

"We should have ordered wine," said Katherine.

"I ordered some," said the Lieutenant.

"You have the most charming accent," Katherine said. "Have I said that already?"

"No," said the Lieutenant, "but thank you."

"I could listen to you talk all day long," she said.

"I'm sure that's not true," said the Lieutenant.

"I mean it," she said. "I mean every word I say. I think your accent is the most charming thing in this whole charming little town." She laughed and then hiccuped, softly, into her fist. The Lieutenant began to talk about the town's principal features, things we should be sure to see, and I was grateful to him for talking so that I didn't have to but also bored by what he was saying, and I stopped paying attention. I listened instead to Katherine cooing over everything he said. The waiter brought the wine and then our food. I wasn't very hungry but I ate to have something to do and so I could think about something else. Then we had finished and Katherine said that she felt tired and would like to lie down. She invited the Lieutenant to join us for dinner and he said that he would be happy to, if I didn't mind, and that he would come up to the hotel around dinnertime. We stood and shook hands and I watched him cross the square, standing straight and walking with precision in his neat uniform.

Katherine said, "Did you enjoy that? Are you proud?"

"I don't know what you mean," I said.

"Do you think it was pleasant for everyone, with you sulking?"

"I wasn't sulking," I said. "I was just
thinking," but she had kept talking while I
was trying to reply.

"Do you think it was easy for me?" she was
saying, but I didn't know what she was exactly referring to, because I had been talking and had missed the middle part.

"You made it look easy," I said anyway.
"You made it look damned easy."

"The poor Lieutenant," she said. "I can't
imagine how he felt."

"I don't give a good God damn how he felt,"
I said.

"You don't give a good God damn how anyone feels," she said. "Or I've forgotten,
haven't I: you're the only one who feels
anything at all." She looked around to see if
anyone had noticed us fighting. "I want to go
back to the hotel," she said. "Will you walk
me back to the hotel? Will you do that much?
I won't ask anything else of you. I know how
hard it all is for you." She was checking her
face in a mirror she had pulled from her
purse. "You're so sensitive and so wounded,"
she said, looking at herself but talking to
me. "My poor husband the Artist."

"You're being unfair," I said, because she
was drunk and there was no use arguing with
her and the only thing to do was to get her
to stop. "Please stop this. If you want to go
back to the hotel I'll take you, only please
stop this."

She stood up without saying anything else and we left the square. She walked a few feet ahead of me the whole way and I didn't try to catch her or talk to her, but instead tried to see everything along the trip and remember it the way it was so that I could write about it and think about it and so that the things along the walk would be what I remembered and not the fight we'd had, because it wouldn't matter later that we had fought because we were husband and wife, and these things happened. I felt bad that we had fought at all, and felt that I was being very petty, and so when we had walked past the gates and across the lawn into the cool lobby, and then crossed the lobby and climbed aboard the elevator and we were alone inside, I said, "I'm sorry. I'm sorry that I ruined lunch for you. I'll make it up to you at dinner, I promise. I'll be everything you want me to be and we'll talk about whatever you want to talk about because it doesn't matter to me, none of the other things matter to me as much as making you happy."

"You think just because something hurts you that you can go and act in whatever way you want to," she said, all of a sudden. "Well I get hurt, too. Other people get hurt, too, and their hurt matters just as much as yours."

"Where did that come from?" I said. "What does that mean?"

"Never mind," she said. She looked exhausted. "Forget I said anything."

The doors slid open and we walked down the hall together. Once we were inside she went into the bathroom and closed the door, and I sat down on the edge of the bed and waited. It didn't seem to me that she was right at all. I told myself that she was just drunk and that I shouldn't worry about it. After that I felt a little better. I decided to go down to the bar.

"Katherine?" I said. And then, when there was no answer, I called louder and said, "I'm going down to the bar. If you want to talk to me you can come find me there. You can call down to the desk and have them find me." I was putting my jacket back on. Then I went out without saying anything else.

Ten

I went out into the hall and rode down to the lobby, thinking that maybe I would find the other American or Thomas the ski guide, but when I arrived the bar was empty and suddenly I didn't feel like having a drink anymore. I went back across the lobby to the desk and asked if any mail had come in. The clerk reminded me that I had already asked earlier that morning. I told him that I thought perhaps I had asked too soon, and some had been brought up from the train. He told me that he would check again and went to do so. He came back shaking his head. I thanked him and left.

There was hardly anyone on the streets. I looked back over my shoulder at the mountainside and saw skiers coming down and I could see the gondola and the chairs still moving. Down in the square I stopped one of the waiters and asked him where the lodge for the guides was. He looked very tired but was polite and told me that I should go through the square and out the other side and down to where the houses where, and that if I followed the street that he pointed me towards it would take me past the lodge, and that I would know it when I saw it. I thanked him and then I walked through the square and beneath the fountain and came out on the other side. The street beyond the square was crowded and I pushed myself up against a building front and stood, watching them. After a while I noticed a woman watching me from the doorway opposite and when I looked at her I recognized her as the woman I had seen in the lobby that morning. She didn't look away when I looked right at her and so I waited for an opening in the crowd and then hurried across the street.

"Hello," I said, pressing my back against the wall beside the doorway.

"Hello," she said, still looking at me. "I saw you in the hotel."

"Yes," I said. I was watching the crowd. "What is everyone doing?"

"They're shopping for supper."

"Is it always like this?"

"Always," she said. "It's when everyone comes out to see everyone else. I can stand here and see nearly everyone I know, all at once." She was still looking at me. "Are you rich?" she said.

"No," I said, looking at her now. "I'm not rich. Why? Did you think that I was?"

"The only Americans who come here are rich Americans," she said.

"My wife has money," I said. "Her family has money."

"Ah," she said. She nodded like she understood, now. There was a terrific racket coming from inside the building.

"What is this place?" I said.

"This is my father's place," she said.

"What does your father do?" I said.

"Do you want to see? I'll show you if you
want to see." She opened the door and I followed her inside. In the center of the open
room a stone chimney descended into a broad
base, open at waist height and formed into a
basin which glowed orange with the coal
fire inside. The man pulling the bellows'
chain turned to look at us and then shouted
something to his daughter who said, "My father wants to know what you want."

"I don't want anything," I said. "I didn't
mean - ,"

"It's all right," she said, smiling in a way
that made me think she was laughing at me.
"He thinks you're a customer. He wants to
know what it is that you want."

"Oh," I said. The woman shouted something
to her father and he nodded without looking
at her and without taking his hand from the
bellows' chain. "What is he making?" I asked.

"This will be for a shop sign," she said.
"The bakery is getting a new sign. He's making the frame it will hang from."

"Back, please," said her father in heavily
accented English, and I stepped back and he
brought the bar from the coals and laid it
on the anvil. Swinging the hammer he struck
the end, flattening the edge down into a

fanning chisel point. Then, turning it on its side, he beat at the edge with glancing blows, tapering it down until the end of the bar grew long and thin. Then, turning it to the flat again, as the bar turned from orange to dull red, he beat the tip flat and pushed it out, until the end tapered gradually down to a point. Then the heat was gone, and he lifted the bar and set it back in the coals, and set to work on the bellows again.

"This part will be some ornamental leaves and vines that wrap around the frame," his daughter explained. She went over to the frame, which was leaning, partially assembled, against the workbench. "They're going to wrap around here," she said, pointing to the place, "and then up along the top."

"When are they hanging the sign?" I asked.

"Tomorrow afternoon," she said. "Sometime after lunch. A lot to finish by then. The bakery is just down the street. You can come watch."

"I'd like to," I said. "I've never seen anything like this."

"People don't do it this way anymore," she said. "Except shoes for horses. Now there are machines for everything else. The tourists seem to like it, though. It gives them something to look at when they're not skiing."

"My wife was telling me that every twenty-five years the blacksmith has to replace all of the rivets along the pipeline that feeds the fountain," I said, remembering.

"She read about it in a travel book her parents gave us."

"The tourists like stories like that, too."

I watched him for a while. He shaped the bar into a long, thin stem, and formed the end into a leaf, hammering in the veins with a chisel. When that was finished he heated the entire length, running it back and forth through the fire until the whole piece glowed orange. Then his daughter set the partially assembled frame up on the anvil before him and with two pair of tongs he twisted the vine around it. Then he set to work on another vine, and I told his daughter that I would see them tomorrow and I left. Outside I didn't feel like looking for the lodge anymore. I wondered what to do with myself and I couldn't think of anything. I knew that if I could put off seeing Katherine until dinner then I would see her only in the company of the Lieutenant and that she would be all right then and might be all right after. I didn't know how she would be before and I didn't want to risk it. I thought of waiting in the lobby bar, but decided against it. I wanted to sit somewhere and work on the story idea I'd had, but my notes were back in the room and even if I'd wanted to see Katherine I didn't want to walk all the way back to get them. I decided I would do without them, and went looking for a place to work.

Eleven

I never got to work, though, because a little farther down the road I came upon the guides' lodge. It was a long A-frame building with a row of footlockers running along the outside wall. As I approached a van pulled up and Thomas Orestes got out. He opened the rear and a half dozen more men climbed out, their faces all tanned deep brown and with the white rings around their eyes. There were no seats in the van, and looking in I could see boots lined up against one wall and skis and poles laying against the other. The men hurried inside and Thomas and the driver, a shorter man who didn't look like a guide, stayed behind to unload the boots and skis.

"Hello, Thomas," I said, walking over.

"James," he said, "you missed the skiing today! How are you? How is your wife?"

"Fine," I said. "We're having a wonderful time."

"Help with this and then come have a drink," he said. He was unloading the boots. I went over and helped. The driver stood in the

van and handed them out, and we took them
and put them in the footlockers. "We saw your
friend, the other American, today," Thomas
said. "He is improving as a skier, I think." We
finished with the boots and started unloading the skis. We leaned them against the
front of the building in neat columns. "He
lasted much longer today. His wind is improving."

"Did you take him up today?" I asked.

"No," he said, "but I am taking him up tomorrow. We're trading him around." He laughed.
Everything was out and the driver shut the
van and we went inside together. Inside everyone was sitting at low wooden tables
drinking beer out of bottles. We sat down at
one of the tables and someone handed Thomas
a bottle. He said something I didn't understand and the man handed him another. The
driver had one of his own. Someone else said
something I didn't understand and the other
men around him laughed. Then Thomas said
something back. They began to argue, and
Thomas stood up and the other man remained
seated and that was the end of it. Thomas sat
back down.

"I shouldn't be in here," I said. "I'm causing trouble for you."

"I invited you," he said. "You're here with
me. There's no trouble."

"I wouldn't have come if I'd known it was
going to cause trouble for you."

"Please," said Thomas, "it isn't any trouble.
Everyone is just tired."

After that there seemed nothing else to say about it. I finished my beer and then Thomas handed me another and I drank that one, too. He had begun talking to the other men around us, and I couldn't understand what any of them were saying. I sat, thinking about Katherine and about what I was going to say to her to make everything all right again. It was all I had been thinking about since lunch, even though I hadn't realized it until now.

"Thank you for the beer," I said, when that beer was finished, "but I think that now I have to be going. I have dinner plans with my wife."

"All right," said Thomas. "But I'll see you some time soon? You haven't given me one of your stories to read."

"I've got one started," I said. "With some luck I'll have it finished soon."

"Here's to luck, then," he said, raising his beer.

"Luck," said one of the other guides, raising his beer as well.

Outside the sky had darkened and I moved uphill into the corridor between the taller buildings, and then into the square. The waiters were breaking the tables down and carrying them back inside and I watched them and then I was past them into the alley on the other side. When I came out I could see the lights of the hotel and the lights on the lifts above that, and the outline of the peak above it all, silhouetted against the gray-blue sky.

I stopped in the lobby, and asked again if any mail had come. None was at the desk, and so I asked the man at the desk if perhaps any had been brought up to our room. He said that he didn't know, but that none had been taken up while he'd been there. He called to another man and asked him. That man said that he didn't know, either. I thanked them both and crossed to the elevators without saying anything to anyone else. In our room the shower was running so I sat down on the bed and waited. While I sat I looked around to see if there was any mail, but I didn't see any. I went over to the bureau and took out my notebook. I opened it to the last page I had written and read over it a few times. After I had read it I had the feeling that more was coming and so I sat and began to write. Then after a while I heard the shower turn off, and the sound of Katherine's footsteps on the tiled floor, and I closed the notebook and stowed it away inside my luggage. Then I went back and sat down on the bed. A moment later she came out, drying her hair with a towel with another one wrapped around her. She glanced up and me and said, "Is that what you're wearing? We're meeting the Lieutenant in half an hour."

"I don't know," I said. "Is it all right?" She looked me over and shook her head, and I took the jacket off and went to the bureau to look for another. "I've been thinking about you all day," I said while I looked. "I went over to the old town. You'd really love it over there. I watched the blacksmith work for quite a while. I was thinking we might go over together tomorrow. If you felt like it." I held up another jacket and waited for her to look at me. When she did she shook her head again and I kept looking. "Anyway," I said, "it was really rather interesting. I think you'd get a kick out of it."

I turned around with another jacket, and when I did Katherine was right behind me. She had come over while my back was turned. She put her arms around my neck and kissed me and when she pulled away she said, "Promise me that we're going to have a pleasant meal."

"That's all I want," I said.

"Promise."

"I promise."

"Thank you," she said. She kissed me again and I felt the towel around her work its way loose between us. "You make me so crazy," she said. "If I didn't love you so much I don't know what I'd do to you."

"I love you," I said. I really meant it, too. The towel was slipping and Katherine's hands were unfastening my belt. "Aren't we going to be late meeting the Lieutenant?" I said.

"Don't worry about the Lieutenant," she said, "he can wait."

Twelve

I excused myself during dinner and had a quick drink in the lobby bar. Dinner was proceeding pleasantly enough, but I'd somehow felt that I would need something stronger than the wine we were drinking to get through it. When I came back I found that in my absence Katherine and the Lieutenant had settled on a plan to meet the following morning and ride the gondola up to the mountaintop. The plan included me of course, Katherine said. I said it sounded fine. Going back to the room after dinner we were the only ones on the elevator, and when the door closed Katherine kissed me high up on my neck, under my ear. In the room we undressed without turning on the lights and I watched her silhouetted against the window as she moved to the bed. I crawled in beside her, reaching out to touch the bumps along her spine down to the rise of her hip. Afterwards I went to sleep and didn't dream, and when I woke in the morning Katherine was still asleep beside me. Including the hotel in New York and the car on the train, and not including the previous morning, when she'd already been up and showering, this was only the third time I'd come out of sleep and found her there.

It was still early, but right away I felt completely awake. I took my notebook from where I'd hidden it in my luggage and went over to the desk. I had a very clear sense of what I wanted to write, and got quite a bit down. A while later Katherine stirred and so I capped my pen and closed the notebook and sat, looking out the window. I hoped that she would see that I was working and go take a shower or go get breakfast or something, and let me go back to it. But after a moment she climbed out of bed and came over and put her arms around my neck. I kept staring out the window, pretending that I was thinking about something else.

"Good morning," she said. "Did you sleep all right?"

"I slept fine," I said. "How did you sleep?"

"I slept wonderfully. Have you been up long?"

"A little while."

"What have you been doing?"

"Not much. Watching the skiers."

"You and your skiers," she said. "I adore you, Jim. Did you write anything?"

"No," I said. "Yes. Not really. The beginning of something."

"That's wonderful." She yawned. "What time is it?"

"Twenty to nine."

"We told the Lieutenant we'd meet him at nine," she said.

"I remember."

"Jimmy," she said, playing with my hair, "don't you like the Lieutenant?"

"I like him fine," I said. "What makes you think I don't like him?"

"I can just tell. A wife can tell these things about her husband."

"Fine," I said, realizing it as much as admitting it, but annoyed by her ridiculous statement about a wife knowing these things as much as by her keeping me from working. "I don't like him much. What difference does it make? We've already made plans with him."

"I can tell him something came up," she said. "I can tell him you're not coming."

"You'd love that," I said, not thinking about it before I said it.

"What's that supposed to mean?" She said it like she really had no idea what I meant. I wasn't sure what I meant, either. I just wanted to go back to work.

"Nothing," I said. "I didn't mean anything by it."

"If you don't want to come with us then you don't have to come," she said.

"I didn't say I wouldn't go," I said. She was moving into the bathroom, and I had to raise my voice so she could hear me. "I don't want to make an issue out of this. Please. I want to ride the gondola, I adore the Lieutenant, and nothing would make me happier than spending the whole damn day with him."

"Stay here," she called back. "It doesn't make any difference to me." She came out pulling on a sweater. "I don't want to have another episode like we had at lunch. If you don't want to come then please don't come."

"Now you're just being ridiculous," I said. "Please. You're making something out of nothing. And besides, lunch was only the way it was because you got drunk and left us trying to pretend that you weren't." I shouldn't have said that, and knew it even as I said it. Then I said, "Wait, will you just wait a moment?" because she was already halfway out the door.

"Then why don't you just stay here," she said, pausing in the doorway, "and write your secret little story that no one is allowed to read and that I'm sure anyway no one but you is smart enough to understand. Then you can sit up here by yourself and congratulate yourself about how smart and how sensitive and how misunderstood you are."

She went out into the hall and pulled the door closed behind her. I started out after her, but when I was halfway across the room I thought that I'd better have my key, in case the door locked behind me.. The key wasn't on the nightstand, though, and then I remembered that I hadn't taken it out of my jacket pocket the night before. I found it there and went out., but by then Katherine had already taken the elevator. I hit the button and stood waiting for what felt like a very long time. I felt like a jerk for being in the hallway in my pajamas, and for chasing my wife around, and for what I'd said. Then I thought how there would be people in the lobby, and perhaps the Lieutenant would be there, and how ridiculous I would look. The whole thing annoyed me beyond belief, annoyed me enough that I told myself I didn't care what she told the Lieutenant about my absence. I went back to the room, thinking how ever since we'd started on the trip everything with her had been one headache after another. Then I thought that maybe I'd been wrong about her, that maybe I didn't know what she was really like, and that now I was finding out. I told myself not to worry.

I went back to the desk and read over what I'd written, then I picked up writing where I'd left off. It took me until almost one to write it out, and when I was finished I called down to the desk and asked if they had a typewriter I could use. They said they would send one up and when it arrived I sat down and typed the story straight through, without taking any breaks. That took an hour and by the time I was done I was hungry and happy and had almost forgotten about the fight with Katherine. I folded the story and put it in my jacket pocket, and then I put the notebook in the top drawer of the desk. After that I took a shower and shaved, got dressed, and went downstairs to eat.

The restaurant in the lobby was crowded and I took a seat in a booth with my back to the door. The waiter came and I ordered lunch and after he went away I thought about the story and thought that I shouldn't worry so much because if I could write a story like that then God damn it I could write, because it seemed to me then that the story was the best thing I'd ever written, was the best thing anyone had ever written. After I'd finished eating I went over to the desk and asked if any mail had come for me. The clerk said that none had but that I should check back later, as the mail had not come in yet for the day. I said that I would and then I left and went outside and started walking into town. I had decided that I would go down to the lodge and try to find Thomas, and give him the story to read. I turned and walked backwards and watched the gondola moving in and out of the trees. I wondered if Katherine was on one of the ones that I could see. Then I realized that of course she wasn't. I'd forgotten how much time had passed.

The square was busy, and I moved between the tables with my hands in my pockets, whistling and watching the people. I passed under the fountain and came into the alley. Then I smelled coal smoke, and I remembered that they were hanging the sign today, and I walked a little faster and hoped that I could still catch it, remembering that I had told the blacksmith's daughter that I would be there.

Thirteen

There was a crowd gathered outside the bakery. There was a ladder set on either side of the door, and a board placed between them across the top rungs. There was another ladder set farther out from the door, with another board running from its top rung to the center of the board running across the door frame. A younger man that I didn't recognize and the blacksmith stood on the boards across the doorway while another man, older and wearing an apron, stood on the third ladder. As I watched, the blacksmith called into the crowd, and I caught a glimpse of his daughter as she lifted the elaborate arm the sign would hang from. The crowd all helped her lift, and then the baker and the blacksmith took the sign and the younger man and the baker held it up, secure against the wall, while the blacksmith aligned the holes and then drove long, flat nails through the brackets into the seams in the masonry with his hammer. When he'd driven in all the nails the baker and the younger man let go of the arm and the arm didn't move. Everyone

clapped and then the blacksmith called
something else, and his daughter lifted the
sign. The blacksmith took it and the baker
took the other end, and together they fitted
the eyeholes on the frame onto the hooks
hanging from the arm. Then they let it go,
and it swung from the arm, and everyone
clapped some more. The blacksmith and the
baker shook hands and climbed down. I moved
into the crowd, trying to reach his daughter.
When I got close she saw me and came through
the crowd towards me. She had sawdust in her
hair, and the sawdust was the same yellow as
her hair. There were fresh cuts around the
edges of the sign from where they'd fitted it
into the frame.

"It looks very nice," I said.

"Thank you," she said.

"Listen," I said, "I was wondering if you'd
like to have a drink with me. To celebrate
the sign being finished." Then I stopped
talking, because right then the younger man
came over and put his arm around her shoulders. I didn't think he'd heard me ask her, because he didn't seem to notice that I was
there. He kissed her on the side of her head
and she laughed.

"I'm sorry," she said, still laughing, "but
what were you saying?"

"Nothing," I said. "As a matter of fact, I've
got to be going. I'm supposed to be meeting
someone just now. Congratulations again
about the sign." Then I turned and walked
away without waiting for her to say

anything back, feeling foolish for having shown up. I continued down the street to the lodge, feeling like everyone behind me knew something terribly embarrassing about me.

The lodge was nearly empty. There were no skis out front and when I went inside there were only two other men, sitting in the dark in the back of the room. I sat down at one of the tables and looked at the pictures of the guides that had worked the mountain. The pictures lined the wall three columns deep, and as I followed them down I saw that they had begun on the opposite wall as well. They were all very similar. Then one of the men sitting in back came over to me.

"You want a guide?" he said.

"No," I said. "I was just looking for someone."

"Who were you looking for?"

"Thomas Orestes," I said, badly mangling the pronunciation. "I have something for him."

"He's out," said the man. "You can leave it here. He'll get it when he gets back."

"Is he coming back soon?"

"No," said the man, "he's out all day."

"All right," I said, pulling the folded sheets from my pocket and handing them across. "It's nothing very important, but all the same I'd be very grateful to you if you got it to him."

The man unfolded the sheets and looked them over, one at a time. "You're the writer," he said, folding them back together. "You were here yesterday." I told him that I was. He laughed. "No one knew what the fuck you were doing here," he said, laughing and saying it loud enough for the other man to hear it, who laughed as well. "We all wonder what the fuck is Thomas doing with some tourist? Then after you left he told everyone you were a writer. Ah, a writer! says everyone. Why didn't you say something! He'll write a story about us, and make us all famous!" He laughed again and the other man called something and held a bottle out to the man I was talking to. The man took it and handed it to me. "Have a drink with us," he said. "Who knows, maybe Thomas will come back early."

"Thanks," I said, taking the beer and feeling better about giving the man my story.

Then, as I was sitting down, the door opened and a man and a woman, both in their forties, I guessed, came into the lodge and stood just inside the door, looking around. The man was wearing a suit and the woman was in a dress and heels, and I wondered how they had ended up here, because I couldn't imagine them walking the streets as they were.

"Dotty," said the man, "be a dear and close the door." He had an English accent. They sat down on one of the benches and the man placed a thin volume on the table before him, leaning close down to read in the dim light. "It says here," he said, not raising his face from the book, but speaking rather loudly, "that there's been a guide's lodge on this spot for almost one-hundred and fifty years. Isn't that something, Dotty?" He looked up and saw me. "Hello," he called, "are you American?"

"Yes," I said.

"Hah!" he said. "I knew it from the moment I saw you. Wonderful to be in the company of someone who speaks the mother tongue." He came over and we shook hands.

"What are the Americans doing here?" the woman, who I took to be his wife, asked.

"My wife and I are on our honeymoon," I said.

"Oh my," said his wife, "how wonderful. How romantic! Oh, congratulations."

"And where is your darling wife?" said the man.

"She's riding the gondola," I said. "What brings you?"

"Wives' holiday," said the Englishman. "A bunch of the wives from the club got together and planned out this little trip. Marvelously exciting for all of them, and I don't mind telling you it kept them out of our hair for a good long while!" He laughed loudly, more for his wife than for anyone else. "Of course," he said, "now we actually have to go on the bloody holiday. But you'll find out all about that sort of thing, now that you're a married man." He laughed again.

"Oh you men," said his wife. "We go through the trouble to take you to a perfectly charming mountainside village and all you do is sit around and complain."

"Where are you all staying?" I said.

"In the townhouses," Dotty said. "Simply marvelous. Right on the square. Looking out at that Godawful statue all day." She shivered. "Ah well," she said, "good with the bad, I suppose."

"Quite so," said her husband. "Tell me: what do you do?"

"I'm a writer," I said, feeling somewhat ridiculous for saying it to people who might know something about it and to whom I would have to admit that I had not published anything.

"Really!" The Englishman and his wife were both excited by my answer. "Tell me," he insisted, "have you written anything that I might have written? I'm quite a voracious reader," he added.

"I'm certain you haven't," I said. "I did most of my writing for the college newspaper. Since then I've been working on my novel. I'm still waiting to hear back about it."

"Well, you're still young," said the man.

"I can just imagine that being such a terribly frustrating line of work," said his wife. "Good luck to you."

"Thank you," I said.

"We were just headed out for a drink," said the man. "Would you care to join us?"

"I'm supposed to meet my wife," I said.

"Pity," said his wife, and seemed to mean it.

"Yes," I said. "Well, perhaps I'll see you both around."

"Yes," said Dotty, "perhaps we can take you and your wife to dinner some evening."

"That would be very nice," I said. "Goodbye."

"Cheerio," said the man, more English than ever.

Fourteen

I walked across the square and up past the hotel gates. In the lobby I heard her laugh and I followed it into the bar, where I found her seated in a booth with the Lieutenant.

"James!" said the Lieutenant, standing and shaking my hand, "wonderful that you could make it. Katherine insisted that we call up to the room when we get back and have you down for a drink, but she said you didn't answer the phone and she couldn't imagine where you'd gone. Wonderful that you're here now."

"Yes," I said, "I'm here now."

"Hello, Jimmy," she said.

"Hello, Katherine," I said, sitting in the space the Lieutenant made.

The bartender came over, and the Lieutenant ordered another round of drinks.

"But I'm not done with this one," said Katherine.

"That's all right," said the Lieutenant, "the next one will wait for you until you are." He laughed.

"Tell me about the gondola," I said, not finding his joke very funny.

"Oh it was wonderful," Katherine said. "Oh my God. It was the view from the carriage ride, only a hundred times over." Then she went on for a while describing the view, and the people she'd talked to, and a lot of other things that you couldn't describe but only feel, but wasted your time trying to describe anyway. While she was talking the bartender brought the drinks and when she was finished we all sat for a moment drinking them and not saying anything. Suddenly I wanted very badly to go skiing, wanted more than anything else in the world to go skiing. It was hearing her description of the mountain, but it was something else, too. It wasn't sure what it was, but I was sure enough to know that it was the sort of thing better left unexamined. So instead I wondered if the lodge or the hotel had skis to rent, and if Thomas was free to take me tomorrow. It was a silly thing to wonder, because I was sure Katherine would want to do something else tomorrow, and I knew that she wouldn't let me, and would catch hell if I did and she found out.

After a while the Lieutenant said that he had to be going. Katherine protested but he said that he really had to, and that if we ended up in town again we should come by and visit him, and that Katherine knew where he lived. I thanked him and said that if we were in town we would look him up, but that I wasn't sure if we would get the chance because we were only staying for a couple more days and I was sure there were things that Katherine wanted to do that we hadn't done. It was too bad, he said, and I agreed, and then we shook hands and he left, walking as though he was still in uniform.

"Have you eaten anything?" I asked.

"Nothing since breakfast," she said. "The Lieutenant took me to this wonderful little café up the hill by the gondola. I think we passed it on the carriage." Then she said, "I'm glad we came here. I'm having the most wonderful time."

"I'm glad," I said, still thinking about skiing.

"I think it's good that we can do things on our own and it isn't a problem."

"Of course," I said. "I absolutely agree."

"I think it's important for married people to have their own lives," she said. "After all, it's silly to think that you're going to like to do all of the things I like to do. It's silly to think that after you get married you become some other person. You're still you, of course."

"Of course," I said again. I didn't feel like talking.

"It's wonderful, isn't it?" she said. "I just love it here.".

"Yes," I said. Then we were quiet for a while. I finished my drink, and the bartender came over and asked if we would have another. I looked at Katherine, but she was staring off across the room, and seemed to be thinking about something else. I told him no. He nodded and went away. We sat for a while longer.

"Are you still hungry?" I asked, finally. It startled her when I spoke. She smiled an embarrassed smile.

"Starved," she said.

We ate dinner in the hotel restaurant and afterwards went up to our room. I took a shower and when I came out Katherine was on the bed on her side, facing away from me. I got into bed and lay naked beside her, feeling the warmth of her body and the cold from the water inside the sheets. I kissed her her neck and buried my face in her hair. Then I fell asleep. Sometime later she said my name and I woke up, and I didn't know how much time had passed.

"Jim," she said again, "are you awake?"

"Yes," I said. "What is it?"

"I didn't ask you what you did all day."

"What?"

"I was falling asleep and I realized that I didn't ask you what you did while I was gone. What did you do?"

"Nothing much," I said. "After you left I wrote for a while, and then I walked down into town and watched the blacksmith hang a sign at the bakery. Then I went to the lodge to see if I could find Thomas, you remember Thomas from the other night, but he wasn't there. I talked to some of the guides and an English couple who came in."

"There are gobs of them," said Katherine.

"Gobs of who?"

"The English. There are gobs of them here. They're all here together."

"Yes," I said, "the man said something about it. He said they were all together on a wives' holiday."

"What did you and the English talk about?"

"I don't know. I didn't talk to them for very long."

"Oh."

"I told them I was a writer. Everybody thinks it's so wonderful when I tell them, and then they want to know what I've published."

"Shouldn't they?"

"Yes, but there's more to it than that. It's as though they feel they've been lied to, when I tell them that I haven't published anything. Like I'm not a real writer just because they haven't read anything of mine. Like I'm just making it up."

"Nobody thinks that."

"They do, though. You should see their faces. Every single one of them."

"And what if everyone asked to read what you've written? You wouldn't want them to."

"That's not the point."

"But you wouldn't let them, would you?"

"No, of course not."

"So what difference does it make?" she yawned.

"That isn't the point," I said again, really coming awake. "The point is that I have to prove to every God damned sap on the street that I'm actually a God damned writer just because I haven't published anything. They look at me differently after I tell them. They look at me like what I say and whatever I write isn't any good just because some God damned publisher in some office in New York or Chicago or someplace didn't print it."

"Have you heard anything?" she asked.

"No," I said. "Not unless something came today. I didn't ask after I came back."

"Did you finish what you were writing when I left?"

"Yes. A draft of it. It needs some work."

"Can I read it? Please? Please can I?"

"Don't do that Katherine," I said. "You know how I feel about it."

"You never let me read anything."

"You know how I feel about it."

"I'm not going to say anything mean, Jimmy."

"I know. It's not that. It's just that none of it is finished, yet. None of it's right the way I want it."

"It doesn't have to be, for me. It doesn't have to be perfect for me."

"It has to be perfect for me," I said. "I'm sorry. I really am. That's just the way it is with me." I felt ridiculous for saying it. I told myself that I should just let her read anything she wanted, that it didn't matter at all.

She didn't say anything after that, and sometime later I fell asleep again. When I woke again it was still dark out, and I reached out and felt the empty space where Katherine should have been. I rolled over and saw her sitting at the desk, with the lamp shining down on my notebook in her hands. I knew that I had to get out of bed and stop her. I closed my eyes for a moment, just to get ready. When I woke up again it was morning, and she was gone.

Fifteen

I lay back and listened for the sound of the shower, or the sound of her moving around in the bathroom. When I didn't hear anything I sat up and called her name. There was no reply and so I got out of bed and looked in the bathroom, thinking that maybe she hadn't heard me, or was on the phone with her parents and couldn't answer. She wasn't in the bathroom. I took a shower and got dressed. I thought that maybe she had gone down for breakfast, and so I left a note saying that I had gone to look for her and where I had gone. Then I went out, thinking that I would probably find her in the restaurant.

But she wasn't in the restaurant. I went to the front desk and asked the clerk if he knew her, and if he had seen her. The clerk said that he knew her and would have recognized her but that no, he hadn't seen her. But, he explained, he'd only just taken over for the clerk on the night shift, and perhaps she had gone out before he had arrived. The night shift clerk was still in the back and the new clerk called to him and he came out.

"He wants to know if his wife came by here earlier," said the clerk on the morning shift.

"What does your wife look like?" asked the clerk from the night shift. I described her. "Oh, yes, I saw her," he said when I'd finished. "She came through. I didn't talk to her at all. I'm sorry I cannot tell you more."

"Thank you," I said, and put a bill on the counter. "Have a round of drinks on me."

"It's still early," said the day shift man.

"Not for me," laughed the night shift man. "Have one with me, all the same."

"Just a small one," said the day shift man, "to keep the spirits up."

I thanked them again and went outside. The sky was still pink around the edge of the mountain but the rest had washed out to blue. I started down towards town, thinking that maybe I would find her in the square. I tried to remember if I had heard her leave at all, and at what time it had been, but I couldn't remember. I decided I would walk down to the square and if I didn't see her there I would call back to the room from one of the restaurants, and that if she didn't answer I would call the front desk to see if she had come back through.

The town was beautiful and empty in the early morning. In the square a few waiters stood leaning against the fountain, smoking cigarettes and watching the few people coming down from the buildings. I went into one of the shops and ordered coffee and toast and ate standing in the broad entryway, with one piece of toast in my hand and the other uneaten piece balanced on top of my coffee cup, watching the people going by and hoping to see her. When I was finished I asked the man behind the counter if I could use his telephone to call the hotel, and he led me back around the counter to the phone mounted on the wall above his desk. I called and when the clerk answered I explained who I was and that I'd just been there, asking about my wife.

"Of course," said the clerk. "Have you found her?"

"No," I said. "I'm calling to see if perhaps she came back while I was out."

"No, I'm sorry," said the clerk. "I haven't seen her come back."

"All right," I said. "Listen, can you send this call up to my room? Just in case she came through."

"Certainly," said the clerk. Then I waited, and the line clicked and then started ringing. I waited until it rang five times, and then I hung up.

When I went outside again the sky was blue and there were big white clouds coming up over the mountain and trailing off over the valley. I could see them over the open square and then lost them against the buildings. They were moving fast with the wind. I thought about going back up to the

room and waiting her out, and maybe trying
to work on the story, to make some changes
and write it up again. I didn't want to do
that, though, so instead I walked across the
square and down in between the buildings on
the other side. I walked past the blacksmith's shop and the bakery, and then I spotted the van sitting out in front of the
lodge, and the driver loading in the skis
and poles. I said hello to him and then
walked past him and went inside.

The lodge was crowded, and I stood
against the wall beside the door. One man
stood on a table in the center of the room,
holding a piece of paper and calling off
names. I waited until he was finished, and
then I caught up with him as he climbed
down.

"Is it too late to hire a guide?" I said.
The guides who had been hired were filing
out, while the others dispersed themselves
about the room and sat.

"You don't have the proper attire," he said,
looking me over. "You cannot ski in this attire."

"Yes," I said, "I know that, but I was hoping
that maybe there was some that I could borrow? Or rent?"

"And skis?" he said. "Boots? Poles?"

"I would have to rent them, too."

"We don't rent," he said. The guides who
had been hired were all already outside.

"He can use some of mine," said Thomas. He
had come up behind me while I wasn't looking.

The man with the paper spoke to him and I didn't understand and Thomas responded, and the man looked me over again.

"All right," he said. "You want full day or half day?"

"How late does half day go?" I asked, thinking for the first time about how it would be when I came back and saw Katherine again. Then I didn't think about that anymore. "It doesn't matter," I said, "I'll take the full day."

"And where do you want to go?"

"I don't know," I said. "Where can I go?" I was grinning and couldn't stop.

"You can go front bowls, back bowls, or down the ridge line. Or you can just hire a guide to lead you on the regular runs."

"Where is the snow best?" I asked Thomas.

"The back bowls," he said, "but you have to hike to get out."

"I can hike."

"All right. Back bowls, then."

"I'll tell the van to wait," said the man with the paper.

"Ok," said Thomas, "we have to hurry."

After he outfitted me we went outside and got into the van. Everyone had been waiting for us, and once we were inside the van took off right away. We rode up the hill and past the hotel to the base of the run.

At the base of the run there was a group of men sitting under the sign for the gondola. As we pulled up I saw them stand and start pulling their skis and poles from the

snowbank beside them. Then the van stopped
and we all climbed out. The man with the paper began calling off names, pairing the
guides with their clients. Then everyone was
paired and we went inside and loaded onto
the gondola, and then we started and picked
up speed as we climbed out of the building
and rose to the treetops, with the town falling away behind and the unbroken slope
stretching beneath us.

Sixteen

We came up out of the trees, and Thomas pointed to a notch along the ridge and said, "That's where you ski around from the back bowls and come into the front ones, to get down. You see how high up in the mountainside it is? Once we've skied the back bowls we will have to hike back to that notch. Do you still want to?"

I told him that I did. Above us the heavy white clouds were turning steadily gray. I watched the skiers passing beneath us. Thomas was looking out the window, along the ridge and back down into the bowl. The other clients in the car were talking amongst themselves. I thought about Katherine, and about how horribly irresponsible I was being. If she came back to the room and found my note she would know only that I'd gone down into town to look for her. I imagined her wandering around, trying to find me. It seemed a cruel and unfair thing to do to anyone, especially someone I was supposed to love. But there was nothing I could do about it now. I hoped instead that wherever she'd

gone and whatever she was doing would keep
her out all day, or at least until I was down
off the mountain. Then one of the other clients said that we were coming up to it, and I
looked up and saw the gondola hut ahead of
us. Our car came down and we all got off and
went outside, carrying our skis.

The rest of the group, the ones from the
car ahead of ours, were huddled in a circle,
discussing which runs to take. I followed
Thomas away from the group, up to the catwalk that led off toward the ridge. It was a
long walk, and very tiring in the boots and
with the elevation. Finally we crossed over a
rise and below us the mountain angled down
into a wide skirt of clean white snow. Then
it dropped away and rose again, curving and
funneling into a chute far out to the right,
where the ridge cut the snow and forced it
down.

"We'll ski around this way," Thomas said,
indicating the curve leading into the funnel, "and then slow at the part where it
comes into the funnel, because just after
there is a cliff. We'll ski along the cliff
and then drop down into the next open
stretch. When you reach the trees they will
follow the ridge and try to lead you off
that way," he pointed even further right, to
where I could see the farthest roots of the
mountain curving away, "but you want to stay
left, and find the trail. There's a break in
the trees, so it won't be hard to see. That
trail leads up to the ridge and that is

where we walk back up. Otherwise you are
carried out too far that way, and you have
to walk back up to the trail. All right?"

I nodded and he pushed off and started
across the gradual slope leading to the
drop, cutting turns. I followed, making a wide
turn all the way out to where the ridge began to rise. Then I rode alongside it, watching the exposed rocks as they clipped past
me before I turned and rode the field back
down. I could see him, far out and slightly
below me, making beautiful long turns. I
tucked and turned back into the field, feeling the wind moving past my ears through
the woolen cap he'd given me. The skis ran
smooth and the edges cut clean lines behind
me. Then, opening up, I turned sharp and
headed up the rise towards the ridge on the
other side, shooting up and then coming
alongside him before I lost speed and turned
and ducked down again, shooting clean
across on the empty field. Then, turning more
straight downhill, I opened up and slowed,
making gentle turns, and came up close to
him as we entered the funnel. He slowed and I
slowed too, and we came into the shade in the
narrow passageway where the high sides of
the slope blocked the sun. Then there was a
curve in the trail, and as we came around I
could see white snow and blue sky beyond the
cliff's edge. As we reached it we turned and
skied along it, and then the ledge curved
and made a ramp leading us down onto the
second field. Off to the left I could see the

wide break in the trees and beyond that, to our left, I could just barely see the tips of the gondola poles, poking up above the ridge.

Thomas stopped at the top of the field to let me catch my breath. As I started getting my wind back I thought of asking him if he'd read my story. After we'd unloaded from the gondola and started hiking I'd begun to think about the story so I wouldn't have to wonder about Katherine anymore. I wondered if he'd even received it, if the man I'd given it to had given it to him. I wondered if he'd read it and if he had, why he hadn't mentioned it.

"I don't suppose," I said, "you've had a chance to read the story I left for you at the lodge." Then I said, "I'm only asking because I want to be sure that you got it. It's the only copy I have."

"No," said Thomas, looking down the slope. "Yes, I received it, but I haven't had a chance to read it. They gave it to me this morning. I was going to read it when we'd finished for the day."

"Well then," I said, relieved at least that it wasn't because he hadn't liked it that he hadn't mentioned it, "let me buy you a drink later, and you can tell me your thoughts. Come up to the hotel, and we can talk about it."

"Certainly," he said, still looking down the slope, "but not the hotel. Somewhere else."

"I've only been to one other place," I said, and I said the name of the restaurant where the clerk had sent us to hire a carriage.

"That's fine," he said. "Let's meet there." He wasn't looking at the slope anymore, but now up and behind us at the clouds coming over the peak. The clouds were dark gray and black between. "There's weather coming in," he said. "The temperature has dropped, too."

"I thought I was just cold from standing."

"No," he said. "There's snow coming. We should get down. At least back onto the front bowls. If weather comes in it can be very hard to find our way."

"All right," I said. "I'll follow you."

We turned to start again, and the wind pushed hard and cold against my back. Out ahead the sky was a sheet of gray all the way to the horizon, and the mountain had fallen into shadow. It began to snow. I skied high up onto the side of the ridge and then dove straight back across, headed towards the runoff that led out away from the gondola. As I came broadside to the break in the trees I cut hard left, pushing right, and turned into the trees behind Thomas, and everything was still and the air was alive with growing pines and falling snow.

We pressed on for a while, first pushing ourselves along with our poles and then, when the grade got steeper, climbing with the awkward splayed-kneed stance and leaving fish-ribbed tracks behind us in the snow. Finally Thomas unfastened his skis and I did

the same, and we walked carrying our skis
and poles up the hillside. The snow was coming down much faster now, even in where it
was blocked by the boughs above us. We hurried along towards the growing hum of the
gondola wire. It was hard going, and I had to
stop every few steps to catch my breath. Thomas kept moving, and before long he was far
out ahead of me. Pretty soon I couldn't see
him at all. I could hear the wind in the upper branches. I followed his tracks. Soon the
trail grew even steeper. I held my skis together in one hand and my poles in the other
and set them out in front of me, pulling on
them with each step. Snow fell and collected
on my shoulders and stuck to my eyelashes.
Once I tried to call out, but the sound of my
voice was carried away by the wind.

Finally I came around a bend in the trail
and saw the break in the trees ahead, where
the ridge crested before dropping back down
to the front bowls. I could see Thomas waiting for me, silhouetted against the gray sky.
After what seemed like forever I stuck my
skis into the snow beside him and stood
leaning on them, unable to breath or see
through the black spots flashing before my
eyes.

"That was very good," said Thomas, patting
me on the back. "You did very well. It's a hard
climb, for anyone."

"I'm all right," I said. "I'm all right." I was
getting my breath back. After a while I stood

up and put my skis on. "I'm all right," I said
again.

"All right," said Thomas. He pointed down
to where the trees we had just climbed
through rose around the ridge and fell onto
the face. "If we follow the catwalk down to
the trail it will take us out onto the main
run. That will take us all the way back down
to the gondola hut and the hotel."

The snow was falling in thick flakes and
the world beyond where we were standing was
growing into an indistinct blur of white and
green from the pines and dappled gray.

We had been protected from the wind by
the ridge. Out away from it, moving into the
bowl, the wind pushed even harder against
us, howling loud down the open face and making conversation impossible. We moved down
the catwalk and onto the trail, and then under the gondola wire, with the cars swinging
wildly above us in the wind. After a long
time we came off the catwalk and out of the
trees, and the main run stretched beneath us
and I saw the dim outline of the gondola hut
below, and I took off on my own, no longer
worried about keeping track of Thomas but
only worrying about getting down.

The others were already there, waiting
for us. Thomas rode up and took off his skis.
The other guides stood up when he arrived.
They gathered around him and all started
talking at once. I couldn't understand any of
it. The clients all stood together in a knot,
discussing the weather. I figured that was

what the guides were discussing as well, although I couldn't be sure. I sat down under the sign and kicked the snow from my boots. Then one of the guides went over to the clients, and explained that another run was possible, but it would be best to stay on the most obvious trails, and they would not need guides for that. The clients agreed that the weather looked bad enough to quit. Everyone was in agreement, and one of the guides went inside to call the lodge and have them send the van. The clients shook hands with the guides and then started down the hill, carrying their equipment and walking awkwardly in their boots.

Then the van arrived, and I rode back to the lodge with the guides and returned everything I had borrowed. My legs were already growing sore. The man who had assigned the guides to their clients came up to me and told me what I owed. I asked if I could pay Thomas when I saw him later, as I didn't have any cash on me at the moment. He asked Thomas if it was true that he was going to see me later and Thomas said that it was true and the man in charge said that it was fine. Then I said goodbye to Thomas and the other guides and started the walk back to the hotel. By now my legs were growing stiff and it took me longer than it should have. Snow was accumulating on the ground as I crossed the square, and had already covered the hotel lawn by the time I arrived.

"It must be very bad out," said the clerk, when I came inside.

"Yes," I said, "it's getting there."

"We expected it all winter," the clerk said, "but now in the spring, who knows? The weather does what it does." He shrugged and laughed.

"Has my wife come back?" I asked. I was shaking the snow from my jacket.

"Not that I have seen," he said, shaking his head.

"Has there been any mail?"

"The mail is late," he said. "When the weather is bad, sometimes it doesn't come."

"I see," I said. "Thank you."

Seventeen

I went up to the room. Katherine wasn't there, and there was no note. The note I'd written that morning was still sitting where I'd left it. I took a shower and then lay down on the bed. The shower had made my legs feel a little better, but not much. I was getting worried about Katherine. Then, after worrying about her for a while, I looked at the clock and saw that it was almost time to meet Thomas. I got up and got dressed. While I was dressing I watched the snow falling past the window. Through the snow I could just barely see the gondola. The cars had stopped moving, and the run below it was empty. The snow was falling hard and I thought that the skiing tomorrow would be good if the temperature stayed low and the snow didn't begin to melt. I knew that it didn't matter for me because I couldn't go again, anyway.

By the time I left the snow was deep enough to cover my shoes. The ground was still too warm, though, and the snow underneath was melting and the water was run-

ning along the street. In some spots the water had melted the snow all the way through.
I got to the restaurant and went inside. I
felt tired and I wanted Thomas to tell me
about the story so that I could stop worrying about it. I sat down at the bar and the
bartender came over.

"Hello!" he said when he saw me. "Did you
have a nice carriage ride?"

"Yes," I said, "it was very nice. My wife
particularly enjoyed it."

"And this weather!" he said. "A little late
springs snow for your skiing, eh?" He
laughed. "Your wife was in here earlier, with
the other man," he said. "Did she tell you? I'm
having a special. Half price for the tourists!"

"When was she in here?" I asked. I had been
blowing on my hands, trying to warm my fingers, but when he mentioned Katherine I
stopped and sat up.

"Oh, earlier," he said. "Around noon."

"What other man?" I asked, assuming he
meant the Lieutenant.

"The military man," said the bartender. "I
don't know names. She came in, and then later
he came in, and they had some drinks together. I don't know. When he came in they
moved to one of the tables," he pointed towards the back of the room, "and I couldn't
hear what they were saying." Someone was
calling him away. "Do you want a drink?" he
said. "Beer?"

"Yes," I said, "beer is fine." He poured it and I paid and tipped him and then he went away. I felt much better knowing that she was with the Lieutenant and then, thinking about it, I felt a whole lot worse. The bar was crowded and hot and loud with people talking and laughing. Then a group in the back started singing, all of the men and some of the women, beating their glasses on the table to keep time. When that song was finished they all cheered and clapped, and then began another. While they were singing that one Thomas came in. He sat down next to me and ordered a beer. We couldn't talk because of the noise. Then that song ended, and there was more cheering.

"How are the legs?" Thomas yelled over the cheering.

"Sore," I said. I had bundled up to go out in the snow, but now inside I was much too hot. I wasn't thinking about the story anymore. I was thinking a lot of things that I knew were ridiculous. Somehow I couldn't make myself stop. I really didn't know what she might do, or at least felt certain that I didn't know what she might do. I felt suddenly that I was going to be sick, and so I excused myself and pushed my way through the crowd to the bathroom. Once I was inside, away from the crowd and the noise, I felt a little better. Someone had left the window open, and snow was blowing in and piling up on the sill, and the bathroom was freezing cold. I closed my eyes and put my face up to

the opening and breathed in the cold air.
When I opened my eyes all I could see was
the snow, lit up as it drifted past the
lighted window.

I hadn't noticed it while I was in the
bathroom, but the group had stopped singing.
When I came out I saw them all putting on
their coats and moving towards the door. I
waited in the line and then sat down next to
Thomas as the line moved past.

"Are you all right?" he asked. "Your face
is all red."

"Yes," I said. "Someone left the window
open. It's God damned freezing in there." The
bartender was filling our glasses. "So," I
said, "did you read it?" I was too anxious to
be patient. I just wanted to hear what he had
to say so I could go and see about Katherine.
But of course, there was nothing to see about
and no where to go. I knew more, but I still
didn't know anything.

"Yes," he said, "I read it." He took a long
drink of his beer and didn't meet my eyes.
Then, after too long a silence, he said, "what
do I know about these things? My opinion
can't mean anything to you. If I was very
well read, maybe then I might be able to tell
you something."

"All right," I said, already annoyed that
he was being coy about it, "let's say that you
know something about it."

"But I don't know anything about these
things," he said again, still not looking at
me. He took the folded pages from his pocket

and placed them on the bar between us. "What do I know about stories?" he said again. "I don't know anything about stories."

"It's all right," I said, trying to be patient. "If you didn't like it then just tell me that you didn't like it."

"Perhaps it's just that I didn't understand it," he said. "Do you have anything else? I'm sure it was only this one story. I'm certain I would like something else better. This one in particular I felt I did not understand. If I was more well-read I might understand a house under the ocean. To me it meant nothing but to someone who knows books, I'm sure it means very much."

"It doesn't mean anything," I said. "It's just something my wife told me once. It wasn't a reference to anything. And I don't have anything else. It's all back in my desk at home. This one was all I had."

"That's too bad," he said. "Maybe you could send me something."

"Sure," I said, hating him, "I'll send it to the lodge. You can get it there, can't you?"

"Certainly," he said. Then, to change the subject he said, "Did you enjoy the skiing?"

"Yes," I said,

"Will you go out again?"

"Katherine doesn't want me to. And anyway I'm sure I won't have time before we leave."

"You're leaving soon?" he asked.

"Pretty soon."

"So what will you do when you get back?" he asked.

"I don't know," I said. "If any money comes of it, I suppose I'll keep writing."

"And if the money doesn't come?"

"What the hell," I said, "don't say that. You'll jinx it all up. Oh hell. Say it. It doesn't matter. If the money doesn't come I don't know what I'll do. I'll quit writing. I'll go work for Katherine's father. I'll be another guy in a suit waiting for the train."

"You don't mean that."

"That's true enough," I said, hating him even more, "but I sure as hell am going to quit talking to you about it, whatever happens."

It was a mean thing to say, and right away I felt lousy about it. I couldn't apologize to him, though, so I got up off the stool and finished the rest of the beer, fast, while I was standing. Then I put the money that I owed him, the money I had told the man with the paper I would give him, on the bar next to his glass. He wasn't looking at me, and so I picked up the pages and my coat off the back of the chair and left.

Eighteen

The temperature had dropped considerably while I was inside, and the snow on the streets was fine and powdery and caked hard where the wind blew across it. I covered my ears with my hands to keep them warm. When I stepped out of the doorway alcove the wind hit me in a way that I had not expected and I staggered to one side. I felt more drunk than I had inside the bar. I took another step and hit an icy spot and went down, and came up with snow all down the front of my coat. I let go of my ears to stand up, and the air was so cold that they immediately started hurting. When I put my hands back up to cover them my hands were cold from the snow and they did some good, but not much. Then I leaned into the wind and walked back up to the hotel.

Back in the room I spread the pages out on the desk and read over them. Somehow, in the day since I had written it, the story had changed into a collection of flaws so glaring and obvious that I was amazed I hadn't noticed them before. I thought of myself walking around the town, feeling like a great writer. I was completely ridiculous. I wanted very much for Katherine to be there with me, so that I could tell her how sorry I was for all the ways I had ever given myself leave to act anyway I pleased because I was a writer and an artist. I wanted to apologize for being the fool that I knew I was, the fool I'd been for as long as she'd known me. But she wasn't there, so I got undressed and got into bed.

She came in sometime in the night. The bathroom light came on and I saw her standing in the doorway with the telephone in her hand. Then she was gone inside and the door was closed, and the room was dark again. It occurred with the slow unreality of a dream and I didn't believe it when it was happening and didn't believe it when I awoke until I saw the telephone sitting on the bathroom floor. It was ten o'clock, and she was gone again. I thought that maybe this time she'd left a note, but there was nothing on my bedside table. Then I saw paper on the desk and went to look. But it wasn't a note, it was the story I'd written. The pages were torn along the lines where I had folded them, and then torn again. When I saw that I set about looking for my notebook. I found it in the desk drawer, where I'd left it, but all the pages where the story was written were torn from there as well. I looked through the wastepaper baskets but couldn't find them. I looked through her things, realizing that my looking would come to nothing because if she'd taken the pages then she would have destroyed them by now.

I got dressed in a hurry and went downstairs, hoping that I would find her there. Through the lobby windows I could see water running off the awning, and the whole world outside had the shine of snow melt, and the sky was brilliant blue.

The other American was standing at the counter.

"Hey there, guy," he said as I walked over.

"Hi," I said. "Are you leaving?"

"Yep," he said, "That's it for me. Did you get up skiing at all?"

"Just one run, yesterday, down the back bowls and out, before the weather came in."

"Damn weather," he said. "Was going to be my best day, too. Finally got wise and decided I didn't need those guides. Got two runs in and then had to crap out because of the snow. Some luck, huh?"

"Yeah, some luck," I said. I was looking around for her.

"I think I'll go out to Idaho next year," he said. "I hear the weather in the spring is more stable. They've got just as many runs. More runs, in fact, and there are more of them open later in the season. You don't have to hire a damn guide, either, and everyone speaks your language. You ever been out west?"

"Yes," I said. "Once, when I was younger."

"You're younger now."

"When I felt younger."

"Ah, you got your whole life ahead of you," he said, slapping me on the shoulder. "Tell you what. If you're ever in Chicago, you should look me up." He handed me his card. "Just gimme a ring or something."

"I will," I said, although I haven't and didn't plan to, then. A clerk came over and took the papers he had been signing.

"Your cab is waiting for you," the clerk said.

"Well, see ya later, fella," said the other American, putting out his hand.

"Goodbye," I said, shaking his hand. "It was nice to have met you."

I watched the cab as it started off around the loop and watched it until it passed through the gate and was lost down the road. Then I started back across the room, headed for the restaurant, where I thought she might be.

"Mr. Smith?" the desk clerk called after me, and I stopped and turned back. "Oh good," he said, "I thought that was you. You have a letter. It just arrived. It was supposed to arrive yesterday, but with the storm the mail didn't make it up until this morning. I know you have been expecting something, so I wanted to make sure I got it to you as soon as possible. I was going to send someone up with it, but since you're already here." He held out the envelope.

"Thank you," I said, not looking at him.

"You're welcome," he said, but I had already turned away and started across the room towards the bar.

The bar was empty. There wasn't even a bartender. I set the envelope down and went around and made myself a scotch and soda, being very deliberate about it all and trying not to think about the envelope. When I had the drink made I walked back around and raised my glass to the bartender who wasn't there. Then I took a long drink, holding the envelope up and to the side so that I could see it while I was drinking. Then I opened it, and after I opened it and read the letter inside I made another drink, and then another, and there were some drinks early on that I was worried I would get caught making, and then there were others later where I didn't give a damn if someone caught me. I read the letter again, and then I put it back in the envelope and put it in my pocket. Some time later I took it out again and straightened all of the edges, flattening them against the bar. I think I might have read it aloud, but I don't remember. I don't remember getting off the barstool, or crossing the room. What I remember next is someone shaking my arm, and thinking for a moment that I was asleep in my bed at home, with my mother waking me up to go to school. Someone was calling my name and it sounded like her voice, but when I opened my eyes Katherine was standing over me.

"Jimmy," she said, "wake up."

"Where am I?" I said, looking at the wood and shadow in front of and around me.

"You're in the bar," she said. "You fell asleep in one of the booths."

"Did I?" I sat up. I was still drunk, but everything seemed sharper and clearer and farther away than it had before. My drink and the letter were sitting on the table. "What time is it?"

"It's nearly four," she said. "Are you all right?"

"Yes," I said. I took a drink. The soda had lost all of its carbonation and the scotch felt watered down from the melted ice. I drank it anyway. "I'm fine," I said. "Where have you been?"

"I needed some time to myself," she said. "I just needed some time to think." She sat down. She looked like she was going to say something, but was trying to figure out how to put it. Finally she looked like she'd given up trying to think how to put it. She still had the air of someone who had rehearsed what she was going to say, though. "Do you ever feel," she said, "do you ever feel like maybe we rushed into things? Like we may have been in a bigger hurry that we needed to be?"

"No," I said, quickly and without considering it. "Is that how you feel?"

"I don't know," she said. "A little."

"Even so," I said, "you might have left me a note or something. You might have told the clerk to tell me where you'd gone. I was

really worried about you. I looked all over
the place. I was even going to call the police."

"I know," she said. "I don't know what to
say except that I'm sorry."

"Well I'm sorry, too," I said. "About everything. Or about. I don't know. I'm certainly
sorry. I hope saying it is enough, even if I
can't tell you what it's for."

"Doesn't it just feel," she said, "like we
were better together before we were married?"

"No," I said, again without considering
what she'd said. Then I said, "I suppose it is
a bit different. All right. You're right. It's a
lot different." I took another drink. "Christ,"
I said, "it's worlds different. We're like two
different people."

"I know," she said. "I didn't think it would
change things so much."

"I caught sight of my reflection in the
elevator doors when we first got here, and I
didn't even recognize myself. I haven't felt
like myself since it happened. I thought it
was just because we were in such a different
place."

"I feel like we've done nothing but argue
or avoid arguing."

"I know," I said. Then I said, "But I still
feel the same about you, even if I don't feel
the same way about myself. Or don't you love
me anymore?"

"Of course I love you," she said. "It's not
about that."

"Then tell me what it's about."

"I don't know what it's about. Something's different."

"You're no different," I said.

"Yes, I am."

"No you're not," I said, even though I knew that she was. "You just think that you are."

"Don't say things like that," she said. "It only makes it worse."

"I don't know what I can say, then."

"Just don't say anything. Just for a little while."

"Fine," I said, "I won't say anything."

We sat, not saying anything for a while. It seemed funny that it could end so easily, without any big scene or final moment. It just didn't seem to work, and there was nothing else to say about it. I put the letter back in my pocket and finished my drink. Right away I wanted another one very badly.

Nineteen

After a while we went into the restaurant and I ordered coffee and drank it black and felt almost too sober to live. Then, a while after that, Katherine asked if I wanted another drink. It was five o'clock, and everyone around us was ordering cocktails. We waved the waiter over and ordered our drinks and when he brought them I raised my glass and said, "To joyous union, and to the promise of the future, and to happiness."

"That's what my father said at the wedding," she said. "I can't drink to that. Please. I'm too tired for irony. It's exhausting and it's not true."

"All right. To truth, then. Or beauty. Or whatever else people give toasts to."

She touched my glass with hers and we drank. The waiter came back and asked if we wanted to order dinner. We ordered and the waiter went away. Once he was gone Katherine said, "I read your story."

"I know," I said. "I saw."

"I'm sorry I did it, now," she said. "I wasn't thinking. I didn't think until I'd already done it."

"It's all right," I said. "I don't care, now. It wasn't much of a story to begin with."

"Do you remember," she said, "the story you gave me to read on the train, back when we were first going together?"

"Yes," I said. "Of course I remember."

"I thought that was the most beautiful story. I was so amazed that anyone could make something so beautiful. Every time I saw you after that I was in awe that something so beautiful could come from someone."

"Thank you," I said. "That's nicer to hear than you know."

"That statue in the square," she said, "do you know about it?"

"No," I said.

"It's Hephaestus," she said. "I looked it up. He was one of the Greek gods. He was their blacksmith. When he was born he was so ugly that Zeus threw him off of Mount Olympus. He fell all day and night, until he landed in the ocean. He hit the water so hard that both of his legs broke, and he would have drowned, except that sea nymphs saved him. But he grew up to make beautiful things. He made a beautiful chair that all of the gods wanted to sit in. But when Aphrodite sat in it, the chair rose off the ground and hovered high overhead. The beautiful chair had been a trick to catch Aphrodite. Hephaestus wouldn't let her down until she agreed to marry him."

"Did she?"

"Yes," Katherine said. "But she didn't love him. She loved Ares, and kept seeing him even after her wedding. Hephaestus found out, and he made a net to catch them. When he caught them together he dragged them before the gods so that the gods could punish them. But the other gods just laughed. They didn't care about Hephaestus." She took a drink and then laughed. "It's stupid," she said, "but somehow I've never felt so sorrier for anyone in my whole life. And he's not even real. What does that say about me?"

"I don't know," I said. "In any case, I wouldn't think too much about it."

"What happened?" she asked. "What happened to you?"

"What do you mean?"

"The story," she said. "Not the one you wrote for me but the new one. The one that you wrote here. I didn't know you were so ugly inside."

"Now you know," I said. "Does it matter anymore? Does it change anything that hasn't already changed?"

"I don't know," she said. "I guess not."

"Why did you tell me that?" I asked. "About Hephaestus. Why did you tell me about him?"

"Oh," she said, and shrugged. "He reminded me of you."

After dinner we went upstairs and got undressed, and Katherine curled against me and I lay awake for a long time, wondering what she'd meant. The next morning we checked out of our room and carried our bags out to the waiting taxi. Then we climbed in, and the taxi passed around the loop and down along the lawn and through the gates. We passed through the square and down through the buildings, and then along past the blacksmith's shop and the bakery and the lodge. Then the road curved down and around a ridge to run alongside a cliff, and the town was cut off by a rise and was gone behind us. Below us I saw the river winding through the rocks, and then the cliffside dove and met the river, and the river grew wide in the place where the ridge to our right diminished and disappeared into the mountain, and the waters from the other side converged with those from the river we followed. We followed this wider river, winding alongside it and crossing over it on wooden bridges. Some time later I saw the train far out and far below us, coming in across the valley. Then the road jogged from the river and cut down into a valley, and I couldn't see the train. We followed the valley down on a road cut through dense forest and then came up over a rise as the road led over the valley wall, and we descended straight down to the station from above. We passed through the gate at the mouth of the road and into the dirt and gravel yard beside rails, and the driver pulled to a stop and got out. Katherine paid and we took our luggage and climbed up onto the platform.

Then the train pulled into the station, and we boarded and found our seats. We had a private compartment, with a window. I sat across from her and tried to think of something to say. But I couldn't, and so I just stared out the window with her.

Across the valley, in the distance, I could see the hazy white and gray of the far-off mountains. Before us the valley stretched off in all directions, and in among the grass grew a flower I had never seen. I watched the flowers swaying until the train whistle sounded, and then I sat back in my seat and closed my eyes. The train lurched and then the wheels began to stick and hold, and when I opened my eyes again the valley outside was moving and then it was only a blur, the grass and the flowers blending together and turning yellow where they caught the sunlight.

We began to come around, following the
tracks, and I knew that we would have to
pass through the mountains on the other
side.

"Jim," Katherine said all of a sudden,
"let's forget it all ever happened. Can we?
Let's just call it strange or cold feet or
anything else. Let's start over now."

Before us a river came into view, snaking
through the field. As we came broadside it
caught the sun and turned brilliant gold,
shining so that I had to squint and look
away. Another river lay beyond it, and then
another. I watched the third as it rose, and
turn white with sunlight, and for a moment I
forgot everything and just let myself believe that we could be happy together, the
way I'd always imagined we could.

"All right," I said.

California

One

We were on vacation in southern California. It was my ten-year anniversary present
to her, and it was her graduation present to
me. I'd just finished graduate school. We'd
spent the entire day on the beach, under one
of the shade umbrellas that the hotel rented
out. Katherine was reading a book by someone
I had never heard of, and I was reading back
through a draft of the novel I was working
on. It was the first serious writing I'd done
in ten years, and I had promised myself both
that I would be merciless in my editing and
that I would not get my hopes up. Katherine
had asked to read it and I'd told her that I
would let her when it was finished, just like
I'd always promised when we were first married and I was still writing quite a lot. I
didn't actually care anymore about waiting
until it was finished, or at least not in the
way I had back then. I was wary of her reading it because it was a story about a man
who felt that he had rushed into marriage,
that he'd been driven by a youthful and un-
realistic concept of love that he had very

quickly grew out of. I'd been careful not to let her anywhere near it. Once, when we were much younger, she'd found a story of mine that had upset her, and she'd destroyed the only copies I had of it. I didn't think she would do that again, but I was still careful to keep it away from her.

I was walking up the beach back toward the hotel. The pool was between the hotel and the ocean, and there were a couple of places around the pool where you could buy beer and a few other kinds of drinks. I'd been drinking beer all afternoon and all vacation, because I'd been to a doctor who told me to cut back on the harder stuff. I'd been quite a heavy drinker for a number of years, before I went back to school. I'd been working for Katherine's father. I got a beer for myself and a Cuba libre for Katherine. She'd just discovered them, and thought they were the final word in cocktails. I had the drinks in hand and was heading back down to the beach when a girl stopped me.

"What's that you've got there?" she said, pointing at Katherine's drink.

"It's a Cuba libre," I said. "My wife's been drinking them."

"Oh, your wife," said the girl. "I thought you were just really thirsty." She laughed and I laughed too and she said, "Can I try it? I've never heard of a Cuba libre."

"Well, all right," I said. "I guess so. Why not?" I handed her the drink and she took a sip and nodded approvingly.

"I can't blame your wife," she said. "That is terrific."

"Are you staying here?" I said. "I haven't seen you around the hotel or anywhere."

"No," she said, "I live just down the beach a little ways. I just come down here when I'm bored. I like to see if I can get the tourists to buy me drinks. You want to buy me a drink?" She smiled at me. She was still holding Katherine's drink.

"Sure," I said. "You can take that one."

"It's your wife's," she said.

"No, it's all right," I said.

"Well, thanks," she said. "Maybe I'll see you around."

"I hope so," I said.

Two

After that I went back down to the umbrella, wondering just what the hell that had all been about.

"Didn't you get me one?" Katherine said when I sat down, and without looking up from the book in her lap.

"No," I said. "I completely forgot. I'm sorry. I'll go back."

"That's all right," she said. "I've had a million of them already." She closed the book and looked out at the ocean. "I think I'll go in for a swim," she said. "Do you want to join me?"

"I've just got a bit more to get through," I said. "Give me a few minutes and I'll come out." I was holding the pages in my lap.

"Well, I'm going in now," she said, standing. "Come find me when you're through."

"All right."

She started off down the beach and I watched her until she was into the water and swimming out. Then I went back to the pages in front of me. It was a section I had read through a dozen times before, but it

still didn't feel right. I didn't know what to
do to make it any better, though. I couldn't
concentrate, either. I was thinking about the
girl, and feeling ridiculous for the way I'd
acted. I hoped that if I ran into her again I
wouldn't be caught so off-guard. Then I
thought that was a pointless thing to think,
because there was almost no chance I would
run into her again. I was still thinking
about it, though, when Katherine came back.

"I thought you were going to come find
me," she said.

"I was going to," I said. "I got really tied
up in this one part. I'm sorry. I'll come out
now, if you want me to." She was wringing the
water out of her hair.

"I'm going back up to the room," she said.
"I'm going to wash the salt off me before it
dries my skin out."

"I'll go up with you," I said.

"You stay," she said. "We've paid for the
umbrella for the whole afternoon."

"That doesn't matter," I said.

"Stay anyway," she said. "I'm going to call
my parents once I've showered."

"All right," I said.

After she was gone I went back up to the
bar and ordered a double whiskey, thinking
that one once in a while wasn't going to kill
me. I was tired of sitting on the beach and
tired of reading over my own words. I didn't
feel any connection to this novel except
that I'd written it and it was vaguely about
me. Other than that it didn't feel very impor-

tant. I had started it as an exercise and it had evolved into a thesis, and now it was the best long thing I'd written in a long time and since I'd decided that I was going to be a writer again it was the best thing I had going. Even still, I didn't care about it.

At best the novel would be published, and its publication would cause all sorts of problems for me. I would never be able to entirely convince Katherine that it was fiction. She was too sensitive for that and besides, too much of it was too familiar for her fail to recognize it.

I had finished the first whiskey and ordered another, thinking that once in a while had referred to sitting down and drinking rather than one specific drink. When I'd finished my second whiskey I felt that I wanted to go swimming. I set the manuscript with my clothes under the umbrella and walked only a little unsteadily down the beach to the water. Once I was in the water I forgot all about the novel and Katherine and everything else I had been thinking about. I floated for a long time, not thinking about anything. Then I heard people shouting and I swam in to see what was going on. A girl had been held under for too long by the undertow. They'd pulled her out but she wasn't breathing. She lay on the beach, turning blue. One of the hotel employees was working on her. A crowd stood around, holding its breath. Then all of a sudden, in response to what the man was doing, the girl started choking and sputtering and coughing up water. The man who had been working on her rolled her onto her side and she coughed up a lot more water. The crowd started clapping and cheering. Then the ambulance came and took her away. The crowd started to disperse, and a few of the men from the crowd took the one who had saved her over to the bar and bought him a drink.

I got my clothes and the envelope and went up to the room. Katherine was still on the phone, but she was saying goodbye when I came in. She was already dressed for dinner.

"How are your parents?" I said.

"They're fine," she said. "Same as ever. How was the beach after I left?"

"Fine," I said. "A girl almost drowned. When they pulled her out of the water she wasn't breathing at all. One of the hotel employees did CPR, though, and she woke up and started coughing up water. It was incredible.' I was getting undressed. "I've never seen anything so incredible."

"Our reservation is in twenty minutes," she said, "and we're at the mercy of the hotel car service. I wish you'd hurry. If we're too late they'll give our table to someone else."

"I'm getting ready," I said. I was moving into the bathroom. "Did you hear what I was telling you, though? A girl almost drowned. I saw her. One of the hotel employees saved her life."

"I heard you," she said. "They really ought to have a lifeguard on duty, at least on the part of the beach where the hotel guests swim. It was lucky that whoever went down knew what he was doing, but that was just lucky."

"Sure, I guess," I said. She was missing the point, but I wasn't going to argue with her about it. I had more or less given up on trying to make her see things the way that I saw them. I turned on the shower and was grateful for the noise, because it gave me an excuse to not talk to her anymore. I washed the sand from between my toes and out of my hair. I did it quickly, because I knew that if I took too long it would annoy her and make us late, which would annoy her even more.

Three

When I'd finished I came out and found the clothes I was supposed to wear laid out on the bed. It was something Katherine did whenever we were going out for some special occasion, or when there would be people wherever we were going that she knew. She had started by laying out clothes with some new item as the centerpiece, and giving the excuse that she'd bought me something new that she thought would look nice, and she'd only picked out some clothes she thought would go with it. After a while she stopped using that as an excuse and just started laying out the clothes that I already had. Whenever it bothered me I kidded her that I wasn't her son and that we would have to have a child so she could dote on it instead of me. She always laughed, because laughing was her part of the bargain. My part was wearing the clothes she wanted me to wear and acting the way she wanted me to act. She had better social graces than I did, and always had.

I got dressed and as I was finishing
Katherine came back from wherever she'd gone
looking flushed and irritated and so I finished quickly and said that I was ready to
go. In the elevator I asked her what was
wrong and she said nothing was wrong, like
she couldn't understand what would make me
think that something was. The car was waiting for us out in front and Katherine tipped
the concierge and we got in. We arrived in
time to claim our reservation and I kidded
Katherine that she'd been worried for nothing.

"Ten years," I said, when the waiter
brought Katherine's cocktail and my beer. "I
love you today as much as the first time
that I saw you."

"That's sweet," she said. We drank and
Katherine went back to looking at her menu.

"What is it?" I said. "You act like I'm embarrassing you."

"You're not embarrassing me," she said.
Then she said, "I think I'm going to have the
lobster. Have you decided what you're going
to have?"

"I hadn't looked," I said. "You're certain
you're not bothered about something?"

"Nothing at all," she said, with the same
tone she had used in the elevator, like she
didn't know what I was talking about. Then
she said, "There is one thing. When you came
back up from the beach I thought I smelled
whiskey on your breath. But since I know you

wouldn't have been drinking whiskey, nothing at all can be bothering me, now can it?"

"I suppose not," I said, "since I wasn't drinking whiskey. The doctor told me not to, didn't he?"

"He did," she said. "He most certainly did."

"Well then, I couldn't have been drinking whiskey," I said. "Just beer for me." I raised my glass to show her, then took a drink and smiled. She gave a sort of dry, joyless laugh.

"I watched you after you thought I'd left," she said. "I know you went back up to the bar."

"Christ," I said, almost enjoying being annoyed and indignant after sitting for so long, wondering what I'd done wrong. "You're spying on me now, Katherine?"

"It's for your own good," she said. 'It's for your health. You know what the doctor said."

"To hell with what the doctor said," I said. "I feel fine. I know myself better than the doctor does. Besides, it's nothing like it was. I was drinking too much before, and you were all right to say that I was. But it's not like that anymore. I don't know why no one understands that."

"We do understand that," she said, "and we're all glad that you're feeling better. But it just isn't enough that you feel fine. Remember the pictures the doctor showed you. Think about what can happen. They were young men, too."

"Oh Christ," I said again, "can't you all leave me be? I do what you want to do and I say what you want me to say. I wear the clothes you tell me to wear. I spent eight God damned years with your father looking over my shoulder. Haven't I earned the right to do what I want to do with myself? What more can you possibly want from me?" I stood up. "I'm going to the bathroom," I said. "If the waiter comes before I get back order me a steak. I don't care which one. And a manhattan, for Christ's sake. Or whatever you're having. We're supposed to be on vacation." Then I left without waiting for her to say anything. I went into the bathroom and waited in there for a while, thinking that pretty soon she'd get tired of waiting for me and stop watching the door. Then, when I figured that she had, I went out and stood at the other side of the bar, with a post blocking my view of her. I drank another whiskey, thinking that there was no way she'd ordered me the drink I'd asked for, and then one more when I thought about how long it was going to be before I could get another. I paid for the drinks so they wouldn't show up on our bill and then I went back to the table, feeling much better.

"You were gone a long time," she said. "I thought our food was going to get here before you did. Did you walk back to the hotel?"

"No," I said. "I took a walk outside. I needed to cool off." I didn't look at her, because I was sure if I looked at her she would be able to tell that I was lying.

"You're right," she said. "You were right about what you said. Once in a while probably won't kill you. And we are supposed to be on vacation. I don't want to spend my vacation babysitting you and I'm sure that you don't want to spend your vacation being babysat. But promise me that when we get back you'll really give up drinking. You have to promise me."

"I promise," I said, smiling for the first time in what felt like years. "Joyfully, thankfully, I promise. Good God, where's a waiter?"

"Not too much," she said. "Please, remember what the doctor said." The waiter I had waved to was coming over. "Have something mixed," she said, "it's easier on the system if it's mixed in with something else."

"Whiskey and soda," I was saying to the waiter. Then, when he was gone, I said, "Terrific, fantastic. And when we get back, no more drinking. Only beer for me from then on in."

A moment later I saw the waiter coming back with my drink, and I wanted more than anything for it to already be in my hand. Then it was and it was like the first big breath of air after you've swum down too deep.

"Slowly," Katherine said. "Jesus, Jim." She looked away and started playing with her earring. "How did the editing go today?" she said. "Did you get very much done after I left?"

"A bit," I said. The ice in my glass was almost bare and I started looking for our waiter. "I got a bit done. It's all right, I guess. I'm not particularly invested in it. It's nice to have some time with it, though. With everything else I've always been trying to do other things at the same time." I caught the waiter's eye, and held up my glass to show him I need another. "I'm not sure what'll come of it," I went on. "It's just another novel. There are a million novels. I can't imagine why anyone would want to read mine."

"You're not as cynical as that," she said.

"I'm not being cynical," I said, "I'm just being realistic."

"I'm sure your book is very good," she said, "and I'm sure that a lot of people want to read it. I know I want to read it."

"That's what you said about the last one," I said, "and this one is certainly no better than that." I took the glass the waiter handed me and then leaned back to make room for the plate he was setting down. Another waiter had brought Katherine's plate.

"Well," she said, "I still have faith in you."

"Thank you," I said, "that's nice to hear."

Four

Halfway through dinner Katherine started looking like she didn't feel well. I asked her what was wrong and she said that she had a headache. She'd been getting headaches for a few years. The worst one had put her in bed for two days. I asked her if she wanted to go back to the room and she said that she would be all right, but pretty soon after that she said that it was getting worse and that we should probably go. I paid the bill and we took a taxi so that we wouldn't have to wait for a car from the hotel. It annoyed me a little, because the hotel shuttle service was included. There was nothing to do about it, though. Katherine sat very still and rode with her eyes closed and I watched her face, trying to tell how she was feeling. Rushing out like that had sobered me up quite a bit.

Up in the room I gave Katherine two aspirin and then put her in bed. Then I sat for a while at the desk, reading through some more of my novel. A couple of times I thought that Katherine was asleep, but then she would

move in a way that would make me think that
she wasn't. Finally I was pretty sure that
she'd fallen asleep. I left and went down to
the lobby and then outside. The poolside bars
were still serving drinks and I told the
bartender to make me something appropriate
to my surroundings. What he gave me was rum,
I thought, mixed with a couple kinds of juice.
I gave up after the first drink and told him
to just give me a gin and tonic. Then a whole
bunch of people came out of the hotel and
crowded around the bar. I didn't feel like being around them so I started walking down
the beach. There were maybe three or four hotels all in a row, and they all had lights
strung between posts running along the
beach. Then I was past the hotels, and the
light was from the moon shining on the water.

"Hey, Cuba libre," someone called. I turned
around and saw the girl from the hotel bar,
sitting on the front steps of one of the
houses. She was wrapped in a towel and her
hair was wet. "What've you got there?"

"Gin and tonic," I said, holding up the
glass.

"Looks empty," she said. "Want to have one
with me?"

"I wouldn't want to bother you," I said.
"You look busy."

"Funny guy," she said. "You're a funny guy.
Is that a yes or a no?"

"I'd love to have a drink with you," I said.
"Absolutely. Why not?" I walked over and

stood on the beach beneath the bottom step. "What're you having?"

"I'll have to check and see what I've got," she said, standing. "Come on in. I've got to put some clothes on." I followed her inside. "The kitchen's over there," she said, pointing down the hall. "I'd check the freezer if I were you." She went off in another direction and I went down the hall to the kitchen.

"There's nothing in here," I called.

"Then check the cabinet above the sink," she called back. I did. The cabinet was full of bottles. "You find anything?" she said.

"Just about anything you could ever want," I called. "What should we drink?"

"I don't care," she said. "I trust you completely." She came into the kitchen buttoning her jeans. "Whatever you want to drink is OK with me."

"I only know how to make about three things," I said. Then I stopped talking or doing anything else, because the girl's mouth was pressed to mine.

"Anything," she said, when she'd pulled away. "Really. Anything is fine." She went to the cupboards, and after looking for a moment brought down a pair of glasses.

"Are you sure you live here?" I said.

"I'm housesitting," she said. "My friends went to Belize for a year. I haven't been here very long. I'm still getting used to where everything is." She dropped a pair of ice cubes into each glass. "Well?" she said. "Have you decided?" She held the glasses out to me.

"I'll think of something," I said. I took the glasses and set them beside the bottles I had pulled down. She leaned against the counter next to me with her hands in her pockets. I mixed the drinks, trying to watch her without being obvious about it. Then I handed her a glass. "I'm here with my wife," I said.

"I know," she said. She was sliding along the counter, moving in front of me. "You told me at the bar."

"Right," I said, moving to make room for her. "She has a headache. I was just taking a walk."

"I see," she said. She was right in front of me, and I could smell the ocean smell on her skin. "You probably have to be getting back, or something like that."

"Not really," I said. "I mean. I don't know what I mean."

"Don't you love this house?" she said. "The way it's laid out, you can see the ocean from every room. For example, you might not guess it from down here, but the whole wall of the upstairs bedroom is windows. I wake up every morning looking out at the ocean." She took a drink and then said, "Do you want to see it?. It's really a terrific view. It's worth a look."

"I'd love to see it," I said. Then I took the hand that she held out to me, and I followed her upstairs. In the morning I went back to the room, thinking that I would admit everything and let that put the final nail in the coffin.

But Katherine was still asleep when I arrived. I went downstairs and made a plate at the buffet and brought it up to her. She smiled at me without opening her eyes when I said her name. She'd slept straight through the night, and hadn't noticed that I'd been gone.

Jaguar

One

I was on my way out the door to meet Lucy
when Katherine called. She'd had a bad fall
while playing tennis and had hurt her wrist,
although she thought and her friends agreed
that it was most likely only a sprain. In
any case she didn't want to go to the hospital, but she couldn't drive the car with only
one hand. She was still driving the manual
Jaguar her father had given her for her
thirty-fifth birthday. One of her friends
could drive her home, but then the Jaguar
would still be at the club. She wanted me to
come down with the Volvo, which was an automatic, and drive the Jaguar home while she
drove the Volvo. She wouldn't have any trouble with the Volvo, she said, because it was
her right wrist she had sprained and she
only really needed it for shifting. I told
her that I would be down soon and then I
called Lucy and told her that I would have
to cancel because my wife had possibly broken her wrist.

"Oh my God," said Lucy, with the immediate
and sincere compassion that I so admired in

her and loved her for. "Is she going to be
all right? Would you like me to call my father and ask him for the name of a good or-
thopedist? I'm sure he knows a good one. If
you just give me a moment I'd be happy to
call."

"That's perfectly all right," I said.
"There's no need for that." And then I said,
"I'm sorry to cancel on you at the last min-
ute like this."

"No, of course," she said. "Please, don't
think twice about it. Call me later."

"All right," I said. "I love you."

"I love you, too," she said. "I'll see you
very soon."

When I got to the club I found Katherine
in the bar, icing her wrist with her gin and
tonic. The wrist was swollen to twice its
normal size, which for Katherine didn't make
it very large at all. She'd been to the doctor
a week earlier for a physical, and he'd re-
ported another two pounds gone. It wasn't to
the point that he was concerned, he'd told me
over the phone, but it was something worth
keeping an eye on.

"Weight loss is a very common byproduct
of grief," he said, "but it's only tolerable up
to a point. If she loses much more weight I
may recommend that she go on a special diet.
As I said, it's nothing to be concerned about
yet."

I could see, when she lifted the glass to
drink, that the wrist was beginning to
bruise.

"How did it happen?" I asked.

"I tripped," she said. "It was my own stupid fault."

"Do you think maybe you should see a doctor?"

"No," she said into her glass.

"How many of those have you had?" I asked.

"This is the first," she said. "I had one before the match, because I was early. No, I had two actually, because Henry showed up a bit later and he was early, too." She looked at the wrist and winced as she tried to make a fist. "I'm sorry I spoiled your afternoon," she said.

"I didn't have anything," I said. "Just grading papers. I can do that anytime. Come on. I left the Volvo parked in front of the door. I don't want them to tow it."

Katherine gave the bartender our name and the man thanked her and wrote it down on his record. We'd been members at the club for almost fifteen years but the waitstaff changed every season, and no one ever bothered to learn the members' names. We had to give our name every time we ordered something. I'd complained about it to the manager, who had promised me that he would do something about it. Nothing had changed, though. I'd told Katherine not to tip them if they didn't care enough to remember you after you'd tipped them the first time, but she always did anyway. She put five dollars in the bartender's jar. She did it just to annoy me.

There was a laundry truck waiting behind the Volvo when we got outside. I gave Katherine the keys and held the door for her, and as she was getting in the driver of the laundry truck came out pushing the hamper and asked me just who the hell I thought I was, because I was blocking the entire entrance. I ignored him and went to find the Jaguar. I hated driving the Jaguar. I hated everything that reminded me of her father. Hating him, without having to justify it to myself or anyone else, was one of the few luxuries I afforded myself. I was glad that he was dead, because now there was no chance of him ever redeeming himself, although how he would have done that in the first place I have no idea.

Two

As I approached the Jaguar Katherine drove past me, honking the horn. I watched her turn out of the parking lot and when she was gone I went back inside and had a whiskey and then a whiskey with soda because I had to drive. When I was finished I called the bartender over and asked him if he knew my name, or if I had to tell him. I was hoping that he would say he didn't, but of course he remembered me because I'd just come in to get Katherine. I was Mr. Smith, he said, smiling because he'd given me the right answer, and suddenly I liked him even less than if he'd had no idea who I was.

"Congratulations," I said, "one for a hundred. Good for you."

It wasn't really fair to him, because in fact I wasn't really upset with him. I was upset about not seeing Lucy. I'd been seeing Lucy for about eight months, and thought that I was really in love with her. It drove me crazy when I couldn't see her, and it especially drove me crazy that I couldn't see her because of Katherine. Katherine had always

been difficult, but she'd been even worse
since her father died. Her mother was dead,
too. Her mother'd had a stroke a few years
earlier. After that her father had started
visiting all the time. Katherine was an only
child. I had disliked her father before then,
but I wasn't cold enough to enjoy the fact
that he was obviously suffering. After Katherine and I were married, and after the novel
I'd written was rejected by every publisher
under the sun, her father had given me a job
at his company. I always suspected that he
did it to keep an eye on me, although Katherine insisted that it was just because he
wanted to make sure we were taken care of.
That was bad enough, really, because everyone else who'd had to work their way in knew
about it. They couldn't not know. I worked
there for eight years, and by the time I finally got canned I was drinking two liters
of whiskey a week and the doctor said I had
the liver of a man twice my age. Drunk was
the only way I could get through it, though.
I kept waiting around, hoping that her father would retire and thinking that when he
did he would put me in charge, and I could
fire everyone who'd ever looked at me side-
ways. I made it a contest with him, seeing
which one of us would hang it up first. Or
maybe I was seeing how far I could push him
before he would fire me. I was lousy at the
job to begin with, and the more I drank the
worse I got. Katherine finally made it clear
to me the cruelty of the position I was put-

ting her father in, making him choose between firing me, which he should have done for the sake of the company, and making sure that Katherine was taken care of. It's an odd thing, to be asked to look at yourself from the outside when it's you who's causing all the problems and who is the worst sort of screw-up. So we sat down and talked it out. Katherine asked me when the last time I remember being really happy was, and I told her that it was probably when I was in college and writing all the time. I hadn't written anything in almost five years. Katherine's father said that he would work out a severance package, if I put in my resignation, that would cover most of my costs if I went back to school. So I resigned. He beat me but he had to buy me off to do it, which I told myself was something like winning. I went back to school and I wrote another book that was just a compilation of every popular style since I'd written last. I didn't feel anything for it or about it. It felt like a book someone else had written. I wrote it just to write something, just to get back into the feel of writing. Then Katherine read it and said that it was the best thing of mine she'd ever read. She sent it out without telling me and when it was accepted it felt even less like something I'd written. I told the editor to do whatever he wanted to it, and then six months later it came out and everyone loved it. Katherine and I traveled and I did interviews and I stopped drinking so much. I was really happy for eight solid months.

I put the Jaguar into reverse and stalled backing out of the parking spot. I never drove the Jaguar, and I hadn't driven a manual in years. Besides that, the Jaguar had a sensitive clutch. I got it going again and I left the club, hoping that I wouldn't stall again and thinking that once I got Katherine settled in I might be able to run over to Lucy's for an hour or so before her husband got home. I hated forcing the timing. It always almost ruined it for me when I had to keep looking at the clock or worse, when whoever I was with kept looking at the clock. But even if I had to keep looking at the clock, it would still be better than nothing. It really drove me crazy when I couldn't see her. The only time I didn't mind her being with her husband was when I had been with her first. I thought probably Katherine would want to go to bed, and after that I might have some time.

Three

But when I got home Katherine said that her wrist was hurting a lot more, and that she thought she needed to go to the hospital. The wrist was even larger than before and was bruising more noticeably. I told her I'd drive her in the Volvo. On the way to the hospital she told me that she was sorry for all the trouble, and that she hoped she wasn't ruining any plans I'd had for that afternoon.

"I was just going to be grading papers," I said. "It's no trouble at all."

At the hospital we had to wait for almost an hour before they showed us in, and then it was another hour before we saw a doctor. The doctor sent her down for x-rays, and I lost my temper and said that I could have told them that two hours ago, and why didn't they just send her there first? Lucy's husband was home by now, and I knew it. The doctor asked me to lower my voice and assured me that as soon as the x-rays came back he would be right over to see about them.

"Please Jimmy," said Katherine, "it's not worth it. Let's just go where he tells us to go."

We went down to the x-ray room and the tech told Katherine to lie down on a big slab table, and to hold the injured wrist out away from her body. I told her that it was going to be fine and when the tech told me to stand behind the wall I asked him in a voice low enough that Katherine wouldn't hear if there was a phone I could use anywhere nearby. He told me that there was one just down the next hall, but that the x-ray would only take a minute. I stood behind the wall with him and when I asked him what he thought he said that he couldn't say for sure before the film came back, but that from the look of the bruising and the swelling it was probably a break. I looked out through the window at Katherine on the table. She was laying perfectly still, with her arm where the tech had positioned it, held awkwardly away from her body. I knew that she had to be in quite a bit of pain, but you never would have known if from looking at her.

"All done," said the tech. "I told you it wouldn't be long. The film should be ready in ten or fifteen minutes. You can go back up to the ER. The doctor will come find you when the film comes back."

I helped Katherine sit up and then helped her down from the table.

"He says that we should go back to the
ER," I said to her. "He said the doctor will
come find us when the x-rays come back." Then
I said, "He thinks that it's probably broken,
although he says he won't know for sure until the x-rays come back."

"Ask him what they'll do for it if it's broken," she said.

"He already went out," I said. "I'll ask one
of the nurses when we get back to the ER."

We waited another ninety minutes in the
ER. A couple of high school-aged girls came
in who had been in a wreck. Both of them
were crying but neither of them seemed very
hurt. The one that had been driving had a
broken nose from the airbag and the other
was complaining about her ribs. The girls'
parents came in after a while and made a
scene. Everyone was crying and hugging each
other. I sat in the chair in our area reading
a magazine that someone had left. Katherine
sat on the bed, watching the families.

After the girls were treated the doctor
came in to see us.

"I'm very sorry about that," he said. "We
usually have two doctors on this shift, but
the other one's on vacation this week." He
pushed the x-rays up against the light
board. "Yep," he said, "you can see it right
there." He pointed to a sliver that ran next
to the bone of Katherine's forearm, along the
thumb side. We were both looking over his
shoulder. "You did a number on yourself, Mrs.

Smith," he said, in a way that was supposed to sound familiar and, I guess, comforting.

"What do you do?" she asked.

"Well the good news is it's not angulated at all," he said, looking back at the x-ray. "Usually with this kind of break we cast the wrist for four to six weeks, depending on age and a few other factors. How old are you?"

"Fifty," she said, and at first I thought that she couldn't be right, even though of course I knew that she was. "I turned fifty last month."

"Well, happy birthday, then," said the doctor. "Anyway, like I was saying, we'll probably put you in a cast for about five weeks, and then have you come in and we'll get another x-ray and see how you're coming along. If everything looks good we'll just brace it for another four weeks, just to give it some extra support. After that you should be good to go."

"What if it doesn't look good?" she said.

"Well," he said, looking at me, "there are surgical options. But really, that's not worth worrying about at this point. In ninety-nine percent of these cases we take the cast off at six weeks and everything is looking just like we want it to."

"Will I have to shower with a bag over my arm?" she said.

"Yes," said the doctor, laughing because I guess he thought she was trying to be funny.

"When can I play tennis again?" she said.

"I'd give it until after the brace comes off," he said, "but you know what it feels like. When you feel like you can handle it, give it a try. The best way to strengthen it back up is to use it." In the section next to us the girls and the parents were still hugging and crying.

"Can you give me something for the pain?" Katherine asked.

"Sure," said the doctor. "I'll have the nurse bring something in. I'll prescribe something before you're discharged." He was reading through another chart. "Great," he said, finally. "Someone will be in to cast that arm shortly. Right now just try to relax and keep the arm elevated. I'll send the nurse in with some pain meds."

"When is shortly?" I said. "We've been waiting here for three hours already."

"Just as soon as I find them and tell them," said the doctor. "Like I said, we're a little understaffed tonight." This time there was no apology in his voice. He shook my hand, smiled at Katherine, and left.

Four

A while later the nurse came in with two pills and a plastic cup of water. A while after that another man came in carrying a kit. He was younger than the doctor. He spoke in a low voice to Katherine while he was making the cast. I couldn't hear much of what he said. He asked her what the big idea was, going and hurting herself like this. He told her a story about another woman who'd come in with a broken wrist, but I didn't hear enough of it to make sense of it. Then he was finished and he bowed to Katherine as though he'd just finished a performance. She gave him a half smile and touched the tips of her fingers together to show how she would be clapping if her wrist wasn't broken. After he was gone I asked her how she was feeling.

"Tired," she said. "I'm just tired, more than anything."

"I'll go get the nurse," I said, "and see if we can't get that prescription and get out of here." I was anxious to get going. I had remembered while I was waiting that there was

a program on television that night that I
wanted to watch. Katherine climbed down from
the table and gathered up her things. Out at
the nurse's station we had to wait again and
I yelled that we had been there for five
hours already and just wanted to go home.
The nurse told me that there were people
here in worse shape than me, and they didn't
want to hear me yelling about how long I'd
been there. I told her that I didn't need a
lecture, that I just needed the prescription
the doctor had written for Katherine's pain.
The nurse said that she didn't have it but
that she would go and see the doctor about
it. Then the nurse went away and we waited
some more, and even though Katherine didn't
say anything I told her not to start with me,
because I knew she was thinking about telling me that now us waiting my fault.

"I wasn't going to say anything," she said.
She had her jacket on around her shoulders
and was holding the casted wrist to her
breast. I was going to apologize, but I figured that she knew I was only irritated
about the doctors and nurses making us wait,
and that I hadn't meant to snap at her. And
besides, even though I was glad to be there
for her, she had ruined my entire afternoon.

"Sometimes I regret that we never had
children," she said, when the nurse had finally returned, when we'd finally left, when
we were finally going home. "But then I see
something like that, and I'm certain that I
couldn't handle it if we had. I couldn't stand

the feeling of having something so important to you out in the world on its own. I
would lose my mind."

"I know," I said. "I don't know how people
do it." I wasn't really listening to what she
was saying. The program I wanted to watch
was about to start, and I was concentrating
on driving. "It's only gotten more difficult,
too. I see these kids coming through the
classroom still palpably attached to their
parents. You have children staying inte-
grally connected to their parents up
through their early and even mid-twenties.
One hundred years ago kids were leaving
home at fifteen and sixteen years old, com-
municating with their parents once a year
through a semi-unreliable postal service."

I was talking without paying much attention to what I was saying. After a few years
of teaching I'd realized that if I was knowledgeable about a subject I could simply open
my mouth and words would come out that
sounded just like engaged discourse. A few
years after that I'd realized, though I'd been
doing it for years, and might have realized
it sooner, that I didn't even have to be
knowledgeable, only sound knowledgeable.
Throughout my career a scene has played out
a number of times in which a student, attempting to speak to me about something I
said in class, discovers that I have no idea
what he or she (mostly she) is talking about.
Being aloof, I decided at a fairly young age,

was easier than, and just as effective as, being charming.

"You were really unbearable in there,' she
said, after I'd stopped talking and we'd been
quiet for a while. "I should have just driven
myself. I knew you were going to be like that.
I don't know why I asked you to take me. I was
doing fine driving the Volvo."

"That's nice," I said. "And you're welcome
for driving you. I didn't have anything else
I was hoping to accomplish this afternoon."
We were almost home, and I was happy because
I'd only missed five or maybe seven minutes
of the program I wanted to see. It was a pro-
gram about the planes they'd used in World
War II. Katherine didn't say anything else so
I didn't, either.

Five

We got to the house and went inside.

"I'm going to have a drink," Katherine said.

"Make me one," I said.

"No chance," she said, "doctor's orders."

"Just one," I said. I wasn't going to argue with her about it, though. I was already moving into the den. The den was what would have been a child's bedroom if we'd had any children. The family before us had used it as a child's bedroom. They'd put a ladder up the wall of the closet to the trapdoor leading to the attic. The attic had been a playroom when we'd bought the house. I climbed up the ladder and got down the bottle and the glass I had stashed up there. The bottle was about half gone, but it wasn't a problem to get more and I had plenty of chances to bring it in, when Katherine was out. I poured the glass about half full and then I turned on the television. I came in right in the middle of an old pilot's story about one of the battles he'd been in. I wished that I had some ice and I thought that if Katherine was doing something in the living room maybe she wouldn't notice if I got a few ice cubes. Then I thought I'd just get a glass of water with ice in it and drink off all the water and reuse the ice. I was surprised that I hadn't thought of it before. I went out into the hall, making sure to close the door behind me so Katherine wouldn't see the bottle or the glass if she walked by.

She was still mixing her drink, having a hard time doing it with one hand. I got my ice and then I finished mixing it for her. She didn't seem grateful. She didn't seem anything. When I handed her the glass she took it without saying anything. It was only when I handed it to her that I noticed how glassy her eyes were. I thought about the fact that she was drinking after taking pain medication, but then I thought that it would probably be fine and she would just conk out on the couch. She took the first sip and then stood there, looking past the lip of her glass at nothing.

"Aren't you going to have one?" she said, finally.

"You told me I couldn't," I said, hoping I sounded appropriately bitter for a fifty-three-year-old man who had to be told what he could and couldn't eat and drink. "You said it was doctor's orders."

"Never known you to turn down a drink," she said lazily. She took another sip, and I couldn't help feeling disgusted by the creases that formed above her lips when she puckered. "In all the years I've known you. I'm not entirely sure," she said, looking at me. Then she seemed to change her mind. "I'm not entirely sure," she repeated, making it the whole statement, and not just the prelude it had been when she first said it.

"You're not entirely sure of what?" I said. I was watching the little film of water that had formed in the bottom of my glass now that the bare ice was starting to melt. "What is it that you aren't entirely sure of? Of what aren't you entirely sure?"

"I've been thinking lately," she said, "about that statue we saw on our honeymoon. Do you remember the one? It was down in the middle of that little square."

"Sure," I said. "It wasn't a statue, really. It was the fountain."

"Right," she said, "the fountain. You remember."

"What about it?"

"I've been thinking," she said again, "about the guy it was supposed to be."

"Hephaestus," I said. "It was supposed to be Hephaestus, the blacksmith."

"That was his name," she said. "I've been trying to remember it for weeks now."

"Can you get to the point?" I said. I wanted to get back to the pilot's interview.

"I've been thinking that you," she pointed at me with her casted hand, "that you're like Hephaestus, and I'm like Aphrodite. That you tricked me into sitting down in the chair you made, and then I had to marry you."

"Katherine," I said, feeling suddenly exhausted, "I didn't trick you into anything."

"My father was right," she said. "We're too different. We were too young to see it. How long do you think we would have stayed together, if we hadn't already been married?"

"I don't know," I said. "I don't know what the point of wondering is, anyway."

"You're Hephaestus," she said again. "You're an ugly little man who thinks because he's had his feelings hurt he can act any way he wants to." She took another sip of her drink.

"And you're a perfect Aphrodite," I said, "who betrayed Hephaestus by sleeping with Ares."

"Except that I never betrayed you," she said.

"Come on, Katherine," I said. "It doesn't even matter at this point. I know that you slept with that Lieutenant."

"But I never slept with him" she said. "I never slept with him."

"It doesn't even matter that you won't admit it," I said. "I know. I've known for thirty years. Did you think that I didn't know? It's absolutely absurd to think that I wouldn't know. How could I not know?"

"I never slept with him," she said. "I swear on my life I never slept with him."

"I don't care," I said. "I don't want to argue about it. I've made my peace with it. I made my peace with it thirty years ago. When you said let's forget it I forgot it. That was the end of it for me."

"What about that night," she was saying, "what about that night when we were in California? Where did you go all night?"

"What night?" I said, knowing exactly which night she was talking about. "I have no idea what you're talking about."

"Oh yes you do," she said, "oh yes you do."

"No, I don't," I said. And then I said, "You know what, forget it. Just forget all of it. Forget any and all of it." I had stood from the couch, and was calling to her over my shoulder as I walked back to the den. Then I went inside and shut the door, hoping that she would just leave me alone.

Six

I kept watching the show, but I couldn't pay attention to it. After about ten minutes I turned it off and went back out into the living room. Katherine was asleep on the couch, with her head back against the cushions and her mouth hanging open. The glass on the table in front of her was empty and so I went into the kitchen and made her another drink and woke her up with it. She looked confused and then recognized where she was. She took the glass and took a long drink. I sat down in the chair opposite and said, "Are you seriously telling me that you didn't sleep with the Lieutenant?"

"Hmm?" she said, still drinking.

"The Lieutenant in Greece."

"Yes," she said, following me. "No, I never slept with him."

"You can't honestly expect me to believe that," I said.

"I don't have any reason to try to convince you otherwise," she said. "You already assume that I did. Why would I say that I didn't at this point unless I actually hadn't?"

"I don't know," I said. "Because you like to fuck with my head."

"Believe me, Jimmy," she said, "you're too much work to make fucking with any fun at all." She took another sip and I watched the lines in her upper lip. "Don't get pouty on me, all of a sudden," she said. "You're a big boy, now. You can handle hearing the truth."

"The truth about what?" I said. "Your bull-shit about the Lieutenant?"

"No, silly," she said, "the truth about lit-tle old you."

"I know the truth about little old me," I said. "I think I know myself pretty damn well."

"I know that's what you think," she said, nodding. "I know."

"All right, fine," I said. I was completely sick of dealing with her. "Terrific. Fine. You're right. I don't know myself at all."

I went back down to the den and slammed the door. Then I turned the TV on and turned the volume all the way up, because she was yelling something after me and I didn't want to hear it. All the ice in my glass had fused together into one weird-shaped chunk and I drowned it in another pour.

The show was almost over. A panel of old pilots was talking about one particular as-sault. The moderator kept interjecting the facts from the historical account, and the pilots would flesh them out with firsthand details. I finished my drink and had another. The chunk of ice was shrinking noticeably and I knew that pretty soon I would need some more.

After that drink was finished I stood up to go get more ice. I didn't make it out of the room, though, because when I walked past the phone I decided that I should call Lucy. I felt like I had a lot to say to her. I dialed her number, thinking that if her husband answered I would say that I was calling from the census or something like that because hanging up was what people did when they were having an affair, and I didn't want him to get suspicious.

Luckily I didn't have to come up with anything, though, because Lucy answered.

"Hi Lucy," I said. I had to try very hard to speak clearly.

"James," she said. She always called me James. I loved that about her. "What is it? Is Katherine all right?"

"She's fine," I said. "Well, not fine. Her wrist is broken. She's got a cast on it. They think it'll be fine, though."

"What's that noise?" she said.

"Oh," I said. "It's the TV. I was watching this thing about World War Two pilots. I missed a lot of it. It's pretty interesting stuff. Katherine's father was a pilot in World War Two, you know."

"No," she said, "I didn't know that."

"He's dead," I said.

"I know," she said. "I remember when it happened."

"I never liked him," I said. "We never got along. When Katherine and I first got engaged, he tried to pay us off so that we wouldn't get married. He told Katherine that he'd send her on a trip around Europe, and he told me that he'd pay for me to go back to school. All we had to do was not get married right away. All these years I've thought he was a real son-of-a-bitch for doing it. Now I think, shit, he was probably right. If we'd waited we probably would have come to our senses about it."

"James," she said, "Bill is in the other room."

"All right," I said. "Tell him I'm the census man, or something."

"The census isn't until next year."

"Tell him," I said. "Tell him. I don't know. You'll think of something."

"I'll think of something," she said at the same time that I said it. Then she said, "Goodnight, James."

"Goodnight, Lucy," I said. Then I hung up right away because I heard Katherine coming down the hall. I sat back down and pretended that I was still watching the show. The panel was wrapping up, and the moderator was thanking everyone. Then the door opened and Katherine came in.

"I need a ride to the store," she said. "We don't have any food and the medicine is making me hungry."

"What?" I said, turning the volume down so that I could hear her, although I'd heard her the first time.

"Jesus Christ, Jim," she said. She'd noticed the bottle. I'd left it sitting on the table next to the chair. She picked it up and looked at me. "Tell me," she said, "is this a bottle we had, or was this a new bottle when you started?"

"It was new," I said. "One in a series." I didn't care, now.

"Jesus Christ," she said again. I was expecting her to get righteous and indignant and take the bottle, but she didn't. She just looked at me. Then she put the bottle back down and went back out, pulling the door closed behind her. I heard her move down the hall and then I heard the sound of the garage opening and heard her start the car.

Seven

I was sober enough to realize that I was
going to be in trouble when she got back, so
I sat back down and tried to enjoy the peace
I had while she was gone. The show that was
on next wasn't very interesting to me so I
started flipping around and I found an old
movie I hadn't seen in a long time. It was one
I hadn't liked very much, I realized while I
was watching it, but the fact that I had seen
it before when I was much younger made it
interesting. I didn't think at all about what
Katherine had said. After she was gone I
tried not to think about her at all. I
thought about Lucy and wondered if she was
still awake, and just how bad it would be if
I called her again. I had infinite faith in
my own charm. I was certain that no matter
how annoyed she was when she answered I
could win her over. But I didn't call her. I
just watched the movie and kept drinking.
Then I guess I fell asleep in the chair, because I woke up to someone banging on the
front door. They were shaking the whole
house, it felt like. The only thing I could

think was that maybe it was Lucy's husband and he was coming to kill me or beat me up or something like that. I started looking around for a weapon of some sort to defend myself. But when I got out into the kitchen I could see from the lights that it wasn't Lucy's husband. The officer asked if I was the owner of a classic Jaguar. He checked his notes and read back Katherine's license plate number. In the car he explained that she must have lost control because she'd gone off the bridge at a terrific rate of speed. I explained that she'd broken her wrist that afternoon playing tennis and that she probably had trouble operating the shifter with the cast on her hand.

"Might have just gotten distracted, then," the officer said.

"Yes," I said. "I had to drive the Jaguar home from the club, after she fell. She couldn't do it with her wrist hurt. I don't know why she took that car in the first place. The Volvo we have is an automatic."

"I was going to say," said the officer, "that conditions tonight were fine for driving. No ice or rain or anything like that. Accidents like this people either meant to do it, they were impaired, or there was some other strange thing that you wouldn't expect."

"I can see that," I said, agreeing. We were pulling up to the hospital. I'd thought that we were going to the same hospital that we'd been to that afternoon, but the officer had driven me to the bigger one in the next town over. I thanked the officer for the ride and got out. Inside at the nurses' station they weren't sure which room to send me to. Someone said that Katherine was in surgery, and someone else said no she wasn't. Then one of the nurses said that if I would just take a seat in the waiting room then the doctor would be out in a few minutes to talk to me. I went out and one of the nurses brought me a cup of coffee. I guess they could tell that I was drunk. I told myself that nurses were trained to look for that sort of thing, and it didn't mean that I was obvious to anyone else. I was reading a magazine and wondering if the other people in the waiting room could tell that I was drunk when the doctor came out and explained to me that Katherine's skull had been fractured in the crash, and that I wouldn't be seeing her ever again.

"What am I supposed to say to that?" I said.

"Whatever you feel like saying," said the doctor.

"What do other people say?"

"I don't know," he said. "They say a lot of different things."

"Oh," I said. I couldn't think of anything else to do, so I sat back down. I had been reading an article on sport fishing right before he came in, and for some reason right away I wanted very badly to go back to reading it. It seemed like the most important thing in the world. I didn't, though, because the doctor was still standing there, watching me.

"I'll have one of the nurses bring you some more coffee," he said.

"I didn't drive here," I said. "How am I supposed to get home?"

"One of the nurses will call you a cab, when you want to go."

"That's it?" I said. "That's all? What am I supposed to do?"

"Well," he said, "typically people make arrangements, and the mortuary handles everything." He looked really uncomfortable saying it, and for some reason it made me glad to see him looking awkward and unsure of himself. Like somehow it made everything else he'd told me somehow less credible, although of course it didn't.

"You don't know shit," I said, all of a sudden, and for reasons which I could not later recall. "You don't know a God damned thing. Does anybody in here know what the fuck they're talking about?" I was shouting at the top of my lungs. A couple of the nurses came over and took hold of my arms. I was spilling coffee everywhere.

"Sir," one of the nurse was saying in my ear, "sir I need you to calm down."

"What the hell am I supposed to do?" I started yelling. "What am I supposed to do?" Then my knees gave out, but the nurses were still holding my arms. They pulled me up and sat me down in a chair. Everyone else in the waiting room was watching me. I was making

the kind of scene I always hated people making. I pulled myself together. The magazine
was on the floor where I'd dropped it, and I
started thinking about sport fishing again.
I got calm and quiet. I wondered if they
would let me keep the magazine and I
thought that if I just took it no one would
say anything to me because people who where
grieving were allowed to do that sort of
thing. So I picked up the magazine and held
it, rolled over in my hands. The doctor
apologized, but said he had more patients to
see. I didn't say anything to that. After another moment he left. When he was gone I put
the rolled magazine in my jacket pocket.

The nurses had called me a cab, and the
driver came in to get me. When I got home I
looked through the phonebook and found a
mortuary service. There wasn't anybody there,
though, because it was practically the middle of the night. I left a number saying my
name and telephone number, and what the
call was about. Then I sat down and read the
article about sport fishing that I had
wanted to finish. Right away when I was done
reading it I couldn't remember anything
about it. I kept wondering what I was supposed to feel, but I didn't feel anything but
tired. I fell asleep on the couch and woke up
I wondering where Katherine was, and how
her wrist was feeling.

Eight

The funeral was a week later. It was mostly my colleagues from the school, people who hadn't known Katherine but who'd come out to support me, and a few of our mutual friends. I called everyone in Katherine's address book, but a lot of them lived out of state. They expressed their condolences, but couldn't make arrangements on such short notice. Lucy and her husband came, because they'd been friends of ours before Lucy and I started seeing each other, and because they'd both always liked Katherine. Lucy's husband shook my hand and there were tears in his eyes, and I felt like a bastard for sleeping with his wife. Then we had the service, and a few people got up and spoke. Then we carried her coffin outside and loaded it into the hearse. There were more people at the cemetery than had been in the church. Katherine's grave was dug and open. Mine was right beside it, and still closed. The pastor gave the final blessing and they lowered her down. I wanted Katherine to be there, because I felt exhausted and I knew that with her

there I could just be quiet and let her talk
to everyone who came up to us.

Afterwards one of the other professors
had a reception at his house and we stood
around eating and talking about the classes
we were teaching and the students we had. I
had a few who were very bright and a few
who were very talented, and then a lot of
others who wanted to be writers but weren't
either. I said that I never got tired of hearing them tell me how much they loved my
novel and we laughed and then it was like
everyone remembered at once what the novel
was about and it didn't seem funny anymore.
Then people started coming up to shake my
hand and say their goodbyes. Nobody really
wanted to be there. Finally it was just the
host and I, sitting on the couch drinking his
scotch. I was watching his wife carry the
food back into the kitchen, thinking about
how the headstone above my grave had a
nineteen and then a blank space for the
other two digits that would indicate the
year I died. I wondered if I really had fewer
than ten years left, and it struck me that
that would be all right with me. But I knew
that was the way people often felt after the
death of a spouse, and that probably sooner
or later I would start to feel better.

"If there's anything you need," my colleague was saying, "please don't hesitate to
call on us. You know what dear friends you
and Katherine have always been."

"Thank you," I said, realizing that this was his way of saying goodbye, that it was time for me to go, that he wanted me to leave. I stood up and drank off what was left in my glass. "I should be going. You've been more than generous." It was something Katherine would have said in the same situation, and the words felt strange in my mouth.

"Will you take something home?" asked his wife, who'd come into the room for another plate. "There's so much here, we'll never finish it between the two of us."

"That's really all right," I said. "Well, thanks again."

I went to the door and went out without waiting for them to come over and see me off. Outside it was still warm, and I didn't mind walking. I didn't know what to do with myself. I thought about calling Lucy, but I knew that her husband was home. Also, thinking about her made me think about her husband, and the way he had cried when he shook my hand.

When I got home there was a message from my insurance company regarding the Jaguar. Apparently there was some question as to whether the damage had been intentionally caused. They wouldn't be able to complete the claim until the police had concluded their investigation. The agent asked that I call him back at a number he gave. I called the number, but the agent's secretary said that the agent had already gone home for the day. I asked if she would mind taking a message and when she said to go ahead I yelled into the phone that my wife had not intended to fucking drive her fucking car off of a fucking bridge. Then I repeated my name and gave her my telephone number. I hung up without waiting for her to reply and then went to our liquor cabinet to see if we had anything left that was worth drinking.

Nine

I went back to work a week after that. It was the only thing to do. I had been sitting around the house, drinking and watching movies. I would watch a movie and fall asleep on the couch, and in the morning it would be like I hadn't seen the movie at all, because I couldn't remember a single thing about it. I wasn't drunk, I was just thinking about something else the whole time. I went back to work thinking it would help me to get back into some sort of routine. It was what everyone said I should do. They suggested also that I make myself get up and write. I couldn't do that, though. I tried once, but ended up staring at the screen for an hour, waiting for the words to come. None ever did. I wasn't a writer, anyway. I was a professor who'd written a book that only his own students read. I was the kind of writer I'd always looked down on as a student, back when in my mind I was a great writer, one who people would remember.

It was the middle of the semester, and the perfect time to go back. Everything was al-

ready moving along, but without the frantic
scramble that came at the end when everyone
was trying to finish everything at once. I
taught class in the morning and had office
hours in the early afternoon. No one came to
my office hours, though. I suspect they were
worried that if they did they might open the
door and find me crying, or stumble into some
other strange and uncomfortable cavern of
grief from which they would be obligated to
artfully extricate themselves. It wasn't the
case. Back amongst familiar things it was
almost as though the other part of my life
didn't exist. I was allowed to sink unreserv-
edly into my role as teacher. I had only to
recite by rote the hero's progress or the ex-
act role of Jungian archetypes in this or
that piece of fantasy. I didn't have to name
or explicate the specific and layered and
palpable ache of the loss of her. I reclined
in the luxury of the questions behind which
I was allowed always to retreat. What does
this mean, class? What's going on here? What
is the subtext? And what does this imply?

Then, students started coming to see me. It
was all girls at first. They came with cook-
ies or brownies they'd baked in the dorm
kitchens from powder mixes or pre-concocted
dough. It became one of the great pleasures
of my week, watching them stand uncertainly
just inside my door, just barely past the
point where the tiled hallway stopped
against the carpet of my office, holding
foil- or plastic-wrapped plates in their

hands. They'd all written stories they wanted me to read or had questions they needed me to answer. We'd sit and eat and I would recite with unimpeachable authority the answers. Their faces all wore the same expression of pity mixed with admiration. Had they read this novel, I'd ask, or that one? Were they aware of this literary movement, or that philosophical concept? No, they'd never heard of it. They were all young and completely unaware, sparkling with the most enviable kind of ignorance. Then, just as unexpectedly, their attention seemed to turn. It was like watching a herd move across an open plain, all shifting course together and with no discernible impetus. One day they were coming to see me, the next day they weren't. I sat in my office, staring at the blank screen and attempting to write. With the students gone the other half of my life, the life that existed in the space between the walls of our empty house, began to traverse its boundaries, began to stretch like lengthening shadows into my office and classroom, darkening everything. What does this mean, class? And what's going on here? And suddenly the only answer was the two empty places on my headstone where they would list the year that I died. Suddenly the only answer was the wig they'd put on Katherine at the funeral, to cover the noticeable dent in her skull.

Somebody, one of my colleagues, finally told me. It wasn't just that I'd begun to bore them. One of the girls had told her friends that I'd made a pass at her when she'd come to see me in my office. She'd said that I had told her how lonely I was, that I would give her a passing grade if she'd sleep with me.

"That doesn't sound like me," I said.

"How much have you been drinking?" asked my colleague.

"Quite a lot," I admitted, "but only at home. Never at school."

"Anyway, I don't think you need to worry about it yet," he said. "She hasn't filed a complaint against you, which convinces me even more that she's probably making it up. You know how some kids are. The attention. You're just going to have to deal with the rumors for a while. You know how these things go. It would probably be a good idea, though, if you kept your office door open from now on when you've got a student in there."

"Sure," I said. It was almost a moot point, I figured, since no one had been in to see me in more than a week. "Thanks for telling me."

"Not a problem," he said. "And just so I can't say that I didn't ask you: you didn't make a pass at her, did you?"

"No," I said, at least eighty percent sure. I had lied to him about not drinking at school.

"Just checking," he said, shaking my hand. "You're all right otherwise?"

"Sure," I said, knowing that he was already leaving, and not wanting to talk about it anyway. "I'm doing all right."

"You'll have to come over for dinner some night," he said. "Judith puts out a great spread. We'd love to have you."

"Sure," I said again. "Maybe when the semester's over, and I have some time."

I had nothing but time. I sat in my office, waiting for five o'clock. Then I went home and waited for morning. In the morning I waited for class to begin. It was only during class, when I could forget everything and talk and think only about the material, that I didn't watch the hours crawl by. Then I ate lunch in my office, and it started over again. I lay awake at night, waiting to fall asleep. I slept, waiting to wake up. I woke up and started waiting for night, when I could fall asleep again. Life dragged on and on. Nothing else was coming. Everything had ended, but life had continued anyway. I felt like I had run off the edge of the page, into the blankness after the story ends, where everything is concluded and then forgotten. Except whatever was supposed to come, whatever final moment was supposed to occur had failed to occur. I thought about filling Katherine's prescription, about swallowing all of the pills. I thought about hanging myself with my formal faculty gown from the hook on the back of my office door. I thought about jumping from the roof, about splattering on the sidewalk, about the kids running in off the quad. I thought about becoming a rumor, an urban legend, a story about a professor whose life had unraveled and who'd thrown himself in final despair from the roof of the humanities building, where he'd held an office for nearly twenty years. I was a character who'd outlived his story, and now had to do what the author couldn't. I pitied myself with unrepentant leniency and unending patience.

Ten

Three weeks to the day after the rumor started and the sympathetic visits stopped I was sitting in my office staring at the words I'd just written, thinking that they were going nowhere and weren't nearly poetic enough to stand on their own when one of my students, a boy from my beginning composition class, knocked on my door. This boy was particularly memorable to me for his habit of berating the other students in defense of what he took to be the author's "true" intentions, feelings, purpose, et cetera, to which he felt he was especially sensitive and of which, he often asserted, the others were woefully ignorant. He informed these self-righteousness assertions with convenient bits of the author's biography explicated with broad, survey-quality snippets of psychoanalysis and delivered them in a hostile and aggressively condescending tone. Needless to say he was nearly universally unpopular, and might have been something of a headache for me if I hadn't found his observations more than a little insightful on more than one occasion.

"Hi professor," he said.

"Hi," I said, closing the document on the screen without bothering to save what I'd written.

"They say you tried to fuck Grace Hurley," he said.

"That's what they say," I said.

"Did you?" he said.

"No," I said. "I don't know. I don't think so. Look, is that all you want?"

"No," he said. He came in and sat down. "I was wondering if you'd read something. Something I wrote. I've been working on it for a little while. I was hoping you'd tell me what you think." He took a thick manila envelope out of his backpack and handed it to me.

"It feels long," I said, taking it.

"It's pretty long," he said, not quite jaded enough to completely hide his excitement. "Like I said, I've been working on it for a while."

"What's it about?"

"A guy and a girl," he said. "It's a little bit based on something that happened to a friend of mine. The guy and the girl meet at a party and end up driving together to Mexico. Like, on a dare. Neither one of them wants to be the one to chicken out first. On the drive they learn all about each other. I don't want to give too much of it away."

"And what do you think I'll be able to tell you about it, if I read it?"

"I don't know," he said. "Whether or not it's any good. Plus, you're always talking about Kerouac. I though you'd get what I was going for."

"I've got a lot of other work I'm supposed to be doing," I said. "Even if I take it, there's no telling when I'll be able to get to it. If you're looking for a quick response, I can't promise you anything."

"That's cool," he said, standing. "That's totally cool. Whenever. Take your time. Like I said, I've been working on it for a while. I'm not in any big hurry." He zippered his backpack and slung it over his shoulder. 'And by the way," he said, "if you did try to fuck Grace Hurley, I think that's totally awesome. I would absolutely fuck that girl. Rich girls are always into the craziest shit. Daddy issues." He made a face and then broke off, laughing. "All right," he said. "Thanks again, Professor Smith. I'll see you tomorrow.'

When he was gone I took the manuscript out of the envelope and looked over the first dozen pages. There was nothing else to do. I poured myself a drink from the bottle I'd stashed in my bottom desk drawer. That bottle was almost empty, and I made a mental note to pick up another one on the way home.

The writing was just what I expected. Young male writers all tend to have the same hangups. They want everyone else to stand and acknowledge their pain. They don't care who they hurt and they don't feel remorse or regret when they're unfair. Theirs seems to them to be the only story worth telling. Their relationships suffer, because their relationships are only fodder for their misdirected art. They give themselves infinite leeway to affront and offend. Their own sensitivity, their own hurt, seems more than adequate justification to commit any unforgivable betrayal. I read another ten pages and then skipped to the end and read the last ten pages, just to see if I was right about what was going to happen. I was. After that I completely lost interest. I put the pages down and brought up a blank document on the computer. I still couldn't think of anything to say, but I hoped that if I was ready and waiting when the idea came I would be able to get it down correctly.

Thomas Tull lives and works in Cleveland, Ohio. More of his work may be found by visiting www.ThomasTull.WordPress.com. HEPHAESTUS is his first novel.

www.ingramcontent.com/pod-product-compliance
Lightning Source LLC
Chambersburg PA
CBHW020609180626
46810CB00007B/2705